SEEKING MR. PERFECT

JENNIFER YOUNGBLOOD

ARBOR
HOUSE

YOUR FREE BOOK AWAITS

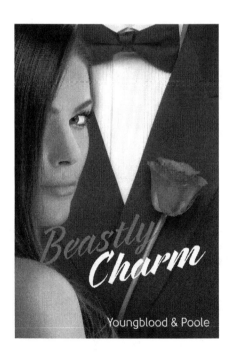

Get Beastly Charm: A Contemporary retelling of beauty & the beast as a welcome gift when you sign up for my newsletter. You'll get information on my new releases, book recommendations, discounts, and other freebies.

Get the book at:

http://bit.ly/freebookjenniferyoungblood

CHAPTER 1

"Tonight's the night." A euphoric laugh rumbled in Sierra's throat as she sat back in her chair and pulled a barbecue potato chip from the bag on the kitchen island. She plopped it in her mouth, letting the tanginess melt on her tongue before chomping, then swallowing. "Parker's taking me to dinner at Rossini's Italian Restaurant in Manhattan, which can only mean one thing—he's proposing." She was so deliriously happy that she wanted to throw open the window and proclaim the news to the neighborhood. All these years, she'd planned and prepared, putting herself in the perfect position to find her real-life Mr. Darcy. And now it was finally happening. She waited for her aunt to respond but there was only silence on the other end of the phone. She leaned forward. "Bennie, did I lose you?"

"No, I'm here."

Bennie's voice sounded weary and worn like an old shirt that had been run through the wash cycle too many times.

Sierra's brows knit together, her voice taking on an edge. "Did you hear what I said? Parker's proposing."

"I heard you," Bennie said dryly. "Are you sure?"

She swallowed, not understanding why her aunt Bennie was acting so prickly. "Well, yeah. Of course I'm sure. Otherwise, I wouldn't be calling you." This was a great day, a day for celebrating. Why was Bennie raining on her parade? "I thought you'd be happy for me." Her voice sounded small and wounded in her own ears.

"Your happiness is my primary concern. I just want to make sure you're making the right decision. You and Parker haven't been together all that long. Maybe you should give it more time, make sure he's the one."

She barked out a laugh. "Seriously? We've been together two years. I think that's plenty long enough for me to know what kind of man Parker is. He's handsome, kind, charming, successful." She could've gone on and on, listing Parker's amazing qualities. Bennie just didn't know him. That's why she was being cautious about the engagement. Sierra had extended a billion invites for Bennie to come here and get to know Parker, but she was always too busy directing her plays and insisted that it was too long of a trek from South Carolina to New York.

"I know all of Parker's qualities," Bennie huffed. "You've told me often enough. From the way you keep carrying on about him, I'm surprised New Yorkers haven't erected a statue in his honor."

Sierra sucked in a breath. "Why're you being so rude?"

Bennie sighed. "I'm sorry, honey. I'm just stressed out of my mind. *Macbeth's* set to open in a little over two weeks, and we're running around like blind squirrels after a fistful of nuts, trying to get everything ready. Freddie Allen's been practicing to play Macbeth for the past three months, and now he's come down with the croup." Her voice trembled slightly. "I don't know what in the heck we'll do if he doesn't get better. Doctor Clarke has given him some heavy-duty antibiotics, but I dunno …" Long pause. "I guess we'll just have to see how it goes. Say a few prayers for us, would ya?"

"I think the Good Lord has more to do than worry about some small-town play," Sierra quipped.

"I—I'm sorry you see it that way." The words tumbled out heavily like soup cans falling from a torn grocery bag.

Guilt twisted Sierra's gut. "I didn't mean it like that."

"I'll have you know this small-town play is very important to the folks of Sugar Pines. Our plays may seem silly and insignificant to you, but we bring culture and refinement to our town—something this world could use more of."

Sierra rubbed a hand across her forehead. "I'm sorry." She needed to learn to think before saying stupid things. The theater was Bennie's life, and she'd just stomped on it.

A strained silence fell between them.

"I really am sorry," Sierra said again.

Bennie let out a long sigh. "It's okay. I accept your apology. Tell me more about tonight."

The false cheerfulness in Bennie's voice hung like a dark cloud over Sierra's head. She no longer wanted to discuss Parker with Bennie. "I'm sure it'll go well," she said evasively.

"This is changing the subject, but Dalton Chandler asked about you the other day."

Sierra jerked, her throat going drier than a week-old biscuit. "What?" she squeaked. "Was Dalton in town, visiting?"

Bennie chuckled lightly. "No, he moved back to Sugar Pines. Bought the Drexel mansion next door."

Sierra clutched her neck. "W-what happened to Steven and Macey Drexel?"

"They moved to a retirement community in Hilton Head, so they could be closer to their kids in Charleston."

Her mind scrambled to connect it all. "And Dalton purchased their house? Can he afford it?"

Bennie chuckled dryly. "Evidently, seeing as how he bought it."

Sierra twisted a lock of hair around her finger, pulling it tight enough to squeeze off her blood supply. "I thought Dalton was still in Seattle. You should've told me." She didn't try to hide the accusation in her voice.

"I thought we talked about this," Bennie said, laughing lightly.

"No, we most certainly didn't." She would've remembered. An image of Dalton with his silver eyes and crooked smile flashed through her mind, unleashing a tumult of conflicting emotions. It was a mistake to call Bennie. Today was supposed to be glorious—the day she would step into her future with Parker. The last thing she wanted was to get dragged back into the past. A past she'd spent the last seven years trying to forget. She balled her fists, her fingernails digging into her palms, replacing the picture of Dalton with Parker.

"I didn't realize Dalton was still such a big deal to you."

Her back went ramrod straight. "He's not!"

"Obviously," Bennie laughed.

Sierra tightened her hold on the phone. "I'm gonna have to let you go." She hated how breathy and desperate the words came out. Why was she getting so worked up over Dalton? So what if he was back in Sugar Pines? The two of them were history. "I have to get ready for my dinner tonight."

Bennie's voice went an octave higher. "Ready for your dinner? It's only eleven a.m. *Jiminy Cricket.* How much time do you need?"

"I know what time it is," Sierra countered, "but I have things to do." She didn't dare mention that those things included shopping for a new dress and getting her hair and nails done. Sierra wanted tonight to be perfect, one she'd always remember, but there was no sense in wasting words trying to explain because Bennie wouldn't understand. She thought Sierra's search to find her own Mr. Darcy was foolish. *As if Bennie had room to talk.* Bennie was the looney one, parading around town in elaborate costumes to get into whichever character she was playing. Sierra had felt like her growing up years were one big freak show. But that was behind her now. She was starting a new life—sane and orthodox.

"I've gotta let you go," Sierra said, looking up as her roommate Juliette burst through the door, her hands loaded with shopping bags.

"Clarissa's Closet is having their semi-annual sale," Juliette exclaimed, dropping the bags in front of the couch as she plopped down and kicked off her stilettos. She sprawled over the couch, sighing loudly. "My feet are killing me," she moaned, sitting up and massaging her toes.

Sierra smiled, shaking her head. Juliette was a hoot—all passion and drama. A rich girl who loved spending as much of her daddy's money as she could. She turned her attention back to Bennie. "Juliette just got home. I need to talk to her before I head out." She was glad to have a pressing excuse to end the call. "I love you." A flood of emotion went through Sierra. Even though Bennie frustrated the heck out of her, Sierra loved her like a mother. She'd raised Sierra from the time she was eleven years old.

"I love you too. I hope all goes well tonight." Bennie paused. "And that you find what you're looking for."

An unexpected pang welted through Sierra as she caught the melancholy note in Bennie's voice and knew she was referring to Dalton Chandler. Bennie considered Sierra's breakup with her ex-boyfriend a tragedy that ranked right up there with King Lear. A trickle of anxiety iced down Sierra's spine. Was it a mistake to marry Parker, when she'd had such all-consuming feelings for Dalton? She shook off the misgivings. No, it wasn't a mistake. Parker was perfect for her—the guy she'd always wanted to marry. Sierra couldn't allow herself to be swayed by Bennie's antics. She'd fought so hard to be where she was now, had to keep her eyes fixed on the future. "Thank you," she said, forcing her voice to sound cheery. "Gotta go," she chirped, ending the call.

Juliette eyed her. "Are you okay?"

A smile shrink-wrapped Sierra's lips. "Yeah. I'm great, actually." She felt a wisp of her former excitement returning. "Parker's taking me to Rossini's tonight."

Juliette's eyes bulged. "Seriously?" Her eyes sparkled as she studied Sierra. "Is it happening?"

A real smile broke over Sierra's lips. "I think so."

Juliette jumped up, squealing. "Ohmygosh!" She rushed to Sierra's side and threw her arms around her shoulders.

Moisture gathered in Sierra's eyes. "Thank you." This is what she'd hoped to get from Bennie—reassurance that all would be well.

Juliette drew back, a mischievous smile tipping her lips. "Have you told your Jane Austen pals yet?"

"No, I tried to call Harley, but couldn't reach her."

"You should post it on the wall of your Facebook group." Juliette's

5

eyes danced. "They'll freak when they hear the news." Her eyes went dreamy. "Jane Austen couldn't have written this any better herself. First, you land that kick-butt account that'll put you on the map in the advertising world, and now you're marrying Parker Henley." She pumped her eyebrows. "*The Parker Henley*, one of New York's most eligible bachelors." She paused. "To think, all those years ago when you went to that girls' camp and made a pact to settle for nothing less than a Jane Austen hero, everything was set in motion." Her lips formed a mock pout as she sniffed. "If I didn't love you so much, I'd be out of my mind with envy."

Excitement bubbled in Sierra's chest. "It is wonderful, isn't it?" she breathed.

"Heck, yeah, it's wonderful." Juliette cocked her head, her hand going to her hip as she gave Sierra the once-over. "Now for the most important question of all … what are you wearing?"

"Well, I thought I'd go shopping and find something."

Juliette brought her hands together. "Fabulous! I'll go with you."

"But you just got back." Sierra's eyes trailed over the mountain of bags on the floor.

"Exactly. Which is why I need to go with you. I know where all the good sales are."

A laugh bubbled in Sierra's throat. "Thank you. You really are a wonderful friend."

Juliette's eyes grew soft and for a second Sierra caught a smidgen of real tenderness before Juliette made a show of dabbing her eyes. "Oh, stop."

She touched Juliette's arm. "Seriously, I appreciate you so much."

A small smile curved Juliette's lips. "You're welcome." She put a finger to her mouth. "Hmm … I'm thinking that with your hair, a green dress might be the ticket. Or blue, to match your eyes."

Sierra thought for a minute. "Definitely green."

"Green it is. What time is your dinner tonight?"

"Parker's picking me up at seven."

A mortified look came over Juliette. "Yikes! We don't have much time. We'd better get cracking."

Sierra smiled at the contrast between Juliette's reaction and Bennie's, feeling vindicated. It took time to put a stylish ensemble together. "I know, I wanna get my hair and nails done if we have time."

Juliette's eyes widened as she hurried over and grabbed her shoes. "Then let's get out of here, pronto!"

As they rushed out the door, Juliette talking a mile a minute about the places they'd go, the last of Sierra's misgivings fell away.

This was right.

Parker was a great catch.

Any girl would be lucky to have him.

And for some strange reason, he'd picked her.

That, alone, was reason enough to celebrate.

CHAPTER 2

hew and swallow, Sierra commanded herself. Her filet mignon was so tender she could cut it with her fork. Too bad she was too keyed up to appreciate it. She placed a forkful of fluffy baked potato in her mouth, then washed it down with water. Candlelight flickered off Parker's handsome face as he flashed a dazzling smile that captured light from the jewels on the chandelier above. He was the picture of perfection in his tailored sports-coat and white-collar shirt. No wonder he'd been named one of New York's most eligible bachelors.

"Are you okay? You seem a little edgy tonight," Parker said, frowning.

A rubbery smile wormed over Sierra's lips. "I'm good." She looked around, her gaze taking in the splendor surrounding them. "This restaurant is incredible."

"I'm glad you like it," he beamed. "It's one of my favorites."

"Oh." She was taken back by his comment, jealousy stabbing through her. Parker had never taken her here before. She wondered who he'd come here with.

"I bring clients here for lunch," he explained, as if reading her mind.

Relief splattered over her as she smiled, feeling foolish. "Makes sense."

They ate in companionable silence until the meal was finished. All the while, Sierra kept thinking how everything was building to the grand finale, which was coming soon ... *she hoped.* Anticipation tingled through her as she took a long sip of water, trying to appear poised on the outside, even though her nerves were jumping like a horde of rambunctious kids, hopped up on sugar.

Parker placed his napkin beside his plate, signaling the end of the meal. Then he leaned back in his seat. "You're probably wondering why I brought you here tonight."

Her heart did a somersault. Somehow, she managed to keep her voice even. "The thought has crossed my mind," she said lightly, placing her napkin on the table.

He reached for her hand, his dark eyes radiating admiration. "I hope you know how much I appreciate you."

"Thanks," she croaked. "I appreciate you too."

"I still can't believe you landed the Pristine Pizza account."

"I had a lot of help from the team."

He nodded. "True. But you're the primary reason Ross gave us the account. He told me that."

"Really?"

"Absolutely."

Ross Snyder owned the fast-growing pizza chain. Wicked smart with business, Ross was a country boy from Alabama who'd grown up hunting and fishing. After moving to Portland, Oregon he started his first restaurant. When he learned Sierra was from South Carolina, an instant friendship was forged. At the end of the negotiations, Ross practically begged Henley Communications to handle his account, with the condition that Sierra oversee it.

"I'm proud of you, Sierra."

The tenderness in Parker's eyes melted Sierra's heart. "Thanks," she murmured.

"I'm officially promoting you to a senior account manager."

Her eyes widened. "That's great." She certainly hadn't expected that. Parker ran a tight ship, only putting the best-of-the-best in managerial positions at his advertising agency. It was flattering to think she was in that category. Also, a raise would be nice.

"That's part of the reason I wanted to bring you here tonight."

Her stomach twisted. Had she totally misinterpreted Parker's intent? Maybe this meeting was solely business. That was the downside to dating her boss—the lines were often blurred between business and personal. She went hot all over, then clammy cold.

Parker released her hand. "And to give you this." He pulled a small rectangular box from his pocket and handed it to her.

Tears glistened in her eyes as her breath caught. Her spirits rebounded instantly. She looked across the table, feeling a rush of adoration for the perfect man sitting across from her. "Is this what I think it is?"

He grinned. "Open it and see."

Happiness poured over Sierra like the morning sun kissing a field of clover. She couldn't stop the broad smile filling her face as she opened the box. A cry wrenched her throat, and she had the feeling of being sucker punched. "Earrings," she mumbled, her heart plummeting. Her chest constricted, making it hard to get a good breath.

"You don't like them," Parker said flatly.

"No … I mean, yes. They're beautiful." She hesitated, trying to figure out how to respond. Her eyes connected with Parker. What did she feel right now? Anger? Hurt? At this point, it was mostly shock. "It's just not what I expected," she uttered, her heart thudding heavily in her chest. Disappointment rolled over her like a tidal wave, leaving a bitter taste in her mouth.

The whites of Parker's eyes popped as realization dawned. "You thought I was going to propose."

Her cheeks went hot. "Well, yeah." She felt like a total moron. A tear escaped the corner of her eye and dribbled down her cheek. Hastily, she swiped it away. Her phone rang. She fumbled in her purse, which was hanging on the back of the chair. It was Bennie. She hit the side button to silence it and shoved it back in her purse.

Parker rubbed a hand across his jaw. "I had no idea that's what you were thinking." He chuckled. "This is awkward."

Anger spiked through her, making her feel nauseated. She glared at him. "What else was I supposed to think? Rossini's is one of the most popular restaurants in Manhattan for marriage proposals."

He spread his hands. "Or to celebrate a promotion, or simply being together." He paused, giving her an apologetic look. "I didn't mean to throw you off. I do want to marry you ... someday."

A harsh laugh scratched through her throat. "When I'm eighty?"

His face drained. "No, in a couple of years."

Her eyebrows shot up. "A couple of years?"

"Yeah, we agreed to take things slow."

"We have been." Her voice rose, catching the attention of the couple at the table beside them. Sierra drew in a breath, trying to calm down. "We've been together two years," she said, lowering her voice.

"I know. And it has been wonderful. Two years from now, we'll know for sure if we want to be together for the rest of our lives."

She had to fight the urge to laugh in his face. As far as Sierra was concerned, they had been taking it slow—painfully slow. Now Parker planned to cool his heels for two more years, saying maybe they'd consider marriage. The whole thing was unbelievable!

Sierra's phone rang again. This time, she ignored it. Her heart was pumping so furiously, she felt like it would fly out of her chest.

"You can get that."

"No," she barked. "It can go to voicemail."

Parker reached for her hand. She tried to pull away, but he held it tight. He peered into her eyes. "I love you."

Tears surfaced. "I love you too."

"I want to marry you. I do. But you know how hard this is for me. Especially considering what happened to my parents."

"Just because your parents got divorced doesn't mean we will," she muttered. Parker's parents had spent several years in a nasty legal battle, fighting over their assets and custody of Parker.

"I know that, but I think we owe it to ourselves to give our relationship plenty of time to mature."

Parker liked to consider all the angles before moving forward. He was that way in business and in his personal life. Sierra knew this about him, so she probably shouldn't be taking this so hard. Still, they'd been together two years. Wasn't that long enough to know if you loved someone? She removed her hand. She needed to get out of here for a few minutes to clear her head and avoid saying something she'd regret. Her phone rang again. She stood, reaching for her purse and slinging the strap over her shoulder. Parker also stood.

"You don't have to get up. I've got to go to the restroom. I'll be right back," Sierra mumbled, walking away.

She held back the tears long enough to get out of the main body of the restaurant. As she walked toward the restrooms, her phone rang again. She cursed, reaching into her purse. It was probably Bennie. Whenever Bennie couldn't reach her, she made a point of calling repeatedly until Sierra answered. However, she was surprised to see that it wasn't Bennie. It was a number she didn't recognize with a South Carolina area code.

"Hello?"

"Hi, Sierra, this is Nadine Thompson."

"Oh, hi." Nadine lived across the street from Bennie. In her younger years, Sierra thought of Nadine as a close friend and mentor. But they'd drifted apart, as Sierra had done with all the people back home in Sugar Pines. This was the first time Nadine had ever called Sierra. She was surprised Nadine even had her number. "Is everything okay?"

"No, I'm afraid not."

Sierra tensed, her throat tightening. "What's wrong?"

"It's Bennie. She's had an accident."

Somehow Sierra managed to find her voice. "What happened?"

"She hurt her knee."

Sierra felt a mixture of alarm and relief. For a second there, she thought something terrible had happened to Bennie. An injured knee was bad, but there were lots of other things that were much worse. "Is she doing all right?"

"She's hanging tough."

"How did it happen?"

"She was on a ladder adjusting the stage lights and fell."

Of all the stupid things to do! "She should've known better than to get up on a ladder," she huffed.

"Yeah, you're right. But you know your aunt."

"Yes, I do," she shot back.

Nadine let out a long sigh. "I'm afraid there's more."

Sierra's heart jumped into her throat as she braced herself.

"Bennie's in over her head financially. She was counting on using the proceeds from *Macbeth* to get caught up on her house loan, but now that she's incapacitated ..." Her voice trailed off.

"What're you talking about?" Sierra's voice was near yelling. A woman walking past gave Sierra a funny look, but she only scowled and turned her back to the woman. "Bennie doesn't have a loan. The mansion is paid for."

Nadine let out a nervous laugh. "Oh, I thought you knew."

"Knew what?" she barked.

"Bennie borrowed against the mansion to fund her outdoor theater."

Heat poured over Sierra as she began pacing—two steps forward, two steps back—in the hall beside the restroom. "How could Bennie be so stupid?" she fumed.

"I'm sorry to put you in a hard position, but it's bad. I can't help but feel responsible because Bennie came to me. I helped her get the loan through The First Federal Bank where I work. I've spoken to the president Leo Farnsworth, and he's willing to give Bennie a thirty-day extension. But if she doesn't get caught up on her payments, the bank will foreclose."

"How far behind is she?"

"She hasn't made a payment in ten months."

She sucked in air. "How much are the payments?"

"Twenty-two hundred dollars."

A headache pounded across the bridge of Sierra's nose. Everything was falling apart faster than she could put it back together. "I can't believe Bennie didn't tell me about the loan. I just spoke with her this morning." Sierra didn't have enough money saved to cover the past-due payments. She'd managed to tuck away a little each month, but it cost a fortune to live in New York. Even with her raise, there would be no hope of amassing the amount of money needed to cover the payments.

"Bennie's too embarrassed to tell you."

Sierra's brows darted together. "Does Bennie know you're talking to me?"

"Heavens, no. You know how much pride Bennie has. She'd let the bank take the mansion a hundred times over before she burdened anyone with her problems. Which is why I had to step in and let you know what's going on."

"I appreciate that. Is Bennie home?"

"Yes, the ambulance came and took her to the hospital. But she was released a few hours later."

Alarm trickled over Sierra. "It was serious enough for an ambulance?"

"I'm afraid so. She did a doozy on her knee. It's swollen up the size of a grapefruit. The doctors say she might need surgery."

"Who's with Bennie now?"

"I went over and spent a few hours, but had to come home and make dinner for Hal. I'll go back over and check on her tomorrow morning."

"She's there? By herself?" The thought of her aged aunt alone with an injured knee in that big house was nearly too much to take. Her own knees went weak. Sierra leaned back against the wall for support.

"Yes, but I'm right across the street. Bennie can call if she needs anything."

"Does she even have anything to eat?"

"I took over a plate of food."

Sierra put a hand to her chest. "Oh, good. Thank you."

"I'm happy to do it. Bennie's like a sister to me."

"I appreciate everything you're doing for her. Thanks for calling and letting me know." She ended the call, her mind on fire. As she stumbled to the restroom, she could only see one option.

She had to go back to South Carolina to sort this thing out. Bennie couldn't lose her house.

CHAPTER 3

oing home was always a mixed bag for Sierra. It was nice to be out of the sweltering heat of the city, back to a landscape as familiar as the back of her hand. Yet, no matter how much time passed or what she'd accomplished, every time she stepped foot across the town limits she was thrown back into the thick of her turbulent childhood. Here in Sugar Pines no one saw Sierra as the adult she'd worked so hard to become. She was simply the niece of the most flamboyant and eccentric lady in town.

This trip was even more nerve-racking than normal because of the situation. She'd talked to Bennie on the phone, demanding to know why Bennie hadn't come clean about her financial problem. Bennie downplayed the severity saying Nadine was overreacting and had no right to call Sierra and stir up trouble. Then she insisted that her knee would be just fine. "You don't worry about me," Bennie said. "I'm doing okay. It'll take a lot more than a bum knee and a pesky bank to get me down."

While Sierra appreciated Bennie's die-hard, self-reliant approach, she obviously wasn't okay. The bank would take her house, leaving Bennie with nothing. Heat prickled up Sierra's neck to the point where she was sure her blood pressure was sky high. She drew in a breath. Freaking out wouldn't help matters. She needed to separate herself from her emotions, think about this rationally.

Fortunately the timing was good, because Sierra needed a break from Parker to process things. Two days after the disastrous dinner Sierra was still smarting. She was embarrassed by her reaction and miffed that Parker wasn't taking their relationship to the next level anytime soon. Furthermore, Parker's reaction to her leaving stung. He was more concerned about making sure Sierra stayed on top of the Pristine Pizza account rather than missing her personally. She assured him that so long as she had her laptop and Internet she'd be able to handle it remotely. She added that contrary to what most New York-er's think, they do have Internet in South Carolina.

As Sierra neared the downtown area of Sugar Pines, she looked at the line of historic buildings with their colorful siding and cheerful windows that looked like bright eyes peeking out. Sabal Palmetto Trees stood in front of the shops, reminding Sierra of tall palm trees.

Her gaze caught on Clydedale's Pizza on the corner with its red and white striped awning. The interior was as cheerful and bright as she remembered. An unexpected warmth flowed through her and she got the feeling she was greeting an old friend.

Even though she couldn't see it from the road, her memory filled in the gaps of the black-and-white checkerboard floor and red-lacquer, swivel barstools lining the counter. She couldn't count the number of times she'd sat in that shop, eating pizza or sipping on a vanilla milkshake, daydreaming about the glitzy future she would create for herself—a future she thought was in her reach before the dinner fiasco.

Next to Clydedale's Pizza was a florist and dry cleaner. The Blankenships used to run the dry cleaner, but Sierra remembered Bennie mentioned that they'd sold it to an out-of-town investment company. The realty company on the end was new. The bakery the same. Her mouth watered, thinking of Ruth Ann's delicate pastries. She made a mental note to stop by there and Clydedale's Pizza in the next couple of days. Sierra had no idea how long it would take to work out an arrangement with the bank, or if that was even possible. But she had to at least try.

Her phone rang. She fished in her purse to retrieve it. It was Parker.

"Hello?"

"Hey, did you get there okay?"

"Yep, I'm about five minutes away from my aunt's house."

"I thought you were going to call me when you landed."

She caught the hint of reprimand in his voice. Was he actually concerned about her? This was new. Maybe she'd been a little too quick to judge him. Her spirits lifted. "Sorry, I didn't have a chance. I was trying to get my rental car taken care of. They lost my reservation."

"Did you get it worked out?"

"Yeah, finally."

"Good."

He sounded distant, distracted. "Hey, this is changing the subject, but Ross called. He wants preliminary ideas about our marketing strategy by this Friday."

She tightened her grip on the steering wheel. That was two days from now. "I thought we had until next Wednesday." She'd be hard-pressed to get something put together by next week, much less Friday.

"Yeah, me too. But he's pushing us to get it to him sooner. You know how these big fish are. They sign a contract and then expect us to jump. I hope you don't mind, but I took the liberty of scheduling a brainstorming session tomorrow at ten thirty. We can patch you in through Skype."

She stopped at a red light. "Okay." She didn't like the idea of Parker going behind her back to schedule a meeting she was supposed to be in charge of. Neither did she like Ross going around her and talking to Parker. Then again, it was Parker's company, so that was to be expected. Then it hit her—the real reason Parker called. To make sure she'd be at the meeting. Disappointment needled through her.

The light turned green. She stepped on the gas. A sign caught her eye as she gasped. Chandler Construction. Was that Dalton's business? She didn't know of any other Chandlers in Sugar Pines.

"What's going on?" Parker asked. "Are you okay?"

It was on Sierra's lips to reply *yes* when her body was thrust forward into the steering wheel. She felt the impact at the same time she heard the loud *pop*, followed by the sickening sound of crushing metal. It went through her mind that she'd rammed into the truck in front of her. Steam rose from the hood of the car, green fluid was spilling from below the glove box. Her mind scrambled to process what was happening. The passenger airbag had deployed from the impact, but not the driver's side. That was probably a good thing. Otherwise, her face would be burned and bruised. Her body trembled as she took an assessment of herself. She was okay. Her knee was a little sore from hitting into the dash. But otherwise, she was perfectly fine. She offered a prayer of gratitude.

She looked at the black Ford truck that she'd hit. *Crap!* Her heart sank. It was a cruel twist of fate that she'd had a wreck, here, in Sugar Pines considering her family history. And she certainly couldn't afford any extra expenses right now. Thankfully, the rental car agent included their insurance in the rental policy. Hopefully, that would cover everything.

Her phone was on the driver-side floorboard. Parker was probably wondering what was going on. She leaned over and retrieved it. The call was still connected. She put it to her ear. "Are you still there?"

"What the heck, Sierra? I heard a loud crash."

She let out a shaky laugh. "Yeah, I hit the truck in front of me."

He swore. "Are you okay?"

"I'm fine." The driver's door of the truck opened. Her gut churned. Whoever was in that truck wasn't going to be happy. *Please let it be somebody I don't know*, she prayed. "Parker, I'm gonna have to let you go. I'll call you after I deal with this."

"But, Sierra—"

She ended the call and rolled down the window, her apology on her tongue. Then she saw him—the one face she'd spent the past seven years trying to forget.

"Dalton," she squeaked. She couldn't breathe! She willed herself to calm down.

He got out of the truck and assessed the damage. Even from this distance she could feel animosity radiating off him. How well she remembered his rugged profile and sharp jawline. His hair was longer all over, hitting just below the ears. Except for the few layers around his face, it was a solid sheet of blonde so dark it was almost brown. On other guys, it would've looked messy and unkempt. But on Dalton, it was sexy. He was dressed in jeans and a black t-shirt that showcased his ripped biceps. She caught a hint of a tattoo peeking out of his sleeve. That was new. He must've gotten that in the military. Dizziness swirled over her as she gripped the steering wheel. She wasn't at all surprised, but still disappointed in herself, when the all-too-familiar attraction simmered in her stomach.

Whenever Dalton was nearby, she felt like he stole all reason from her—stole her very air so that all she could think about was him. She'd told herself that she was a different person now, that her posh city life had immunized her against Dalton Chandler. But now she knew that was a lie. She tried to summon a picture of Parker with his compassionate, brown eyes and sophisticated smile, but it got swept away like a toy boat in a raging river of silvery, blue gray—the color of Dalton's smoldering eyes. Mysterious and brooding, yet so alive … like the tumultuous ocean sky on the brink of a storm.

Crap! He was striding towards her.

DALTON WAS TICKED that some moron plowed into the back of his truck. He'd glanced in his rearview mirror right before it happened and saw the woman on the phone, could tell she was distracted. Then he realized she was going to hit him. In a flash, the scenario played through his mind, but there was nothing he could do. Had he moved forward, he would've hit the car in front of him and the accident would be his fault.

Up to this point, it had been a typical day in the world of construction—the subcontractors begging for more time to complete projects and home owners jumping up and down because the job wasn't done yesterday. Dalton was headed to a job site and realized he'd forgotten some paperwork, so he ran back to his office to grab it. He had a jam-packed schedule today and certainly no time for this. He was supposed to meet the cabinet installers at a new house he was building in less than thirty minutes. Afterward he needed to dart out and meet the building inspector to go over the electrical work for another job. Well, he'd be late now, everything pushed back.

He hurried back to the car, ready to give the woman a piece of his mind. "Lady, I hope you realize what a pain in the butt this is," he began, pushing his hair back from his eyes.

Then she stuck her head out the window, causing him to freeze in his tracks. A single word escaped his throat. "Sierra?"

A rubbery smile wobbled over her lips as she attempted a wave. "Hey."

He shook his head, at a loss for words as she stepped out of the car. She looked good—even better than he remembered. His eyes flickered over her, starting at the bottom and moving up—heeled sandals with her toenails painted bright red, designer jeans that showed just how long her shapely legs were, impossibly tiny waist, and just the right amount at the top. Yep, she still had it—as sleek as a shiny new Corvette, but timeless like his collectible '69 Camaro.

Sierra's hair was longer now with loose waves, flowing like burnished copper over her slim shoulders. He saw the faint dusting of cinnamon freckles over her ivory skin, caught the surprise in her bright blue eyes as she stared back at him. She tucked a strand of hair behind her ear, revealing a gold hoop earring. Memories flowed like a waterfall—how he'd been so gone over Sierra he could hardly form a clear thought, how she'd broken his heart and cast him aside like cheap particle board, not looking back. There were plenty of things he should've told Sierra McCain at this moment. But all that came out of his mouth was, "It's you."

Her faced flamed. "I can't believe I ran into your truck."

He pushed a hand through his hair, still trying to comprehend what was happening. She was here, standing right in front of him like a fairy, or a demon from another world sent to torment him. He glanced at the steady stream of cars slow-poking around them, trying to veer as far from the accident as possible.

Luckily, habit took over. A slow smile stole over his lips, the apathetic one he wore like a pair of sunglasses to hide the pain. "How ya doin', Sie," he drawled.

"Okay." Her expression remained guarded.

His voice took on a good ol' boy drawl. "If you wanted to see me, you could've just stopped by." He cut his eyes at his truck. "Instead of going to all this trouble."

The whites of her eyes popped, and he could tell she was somewhat amused as a half-smile touched her lips. "Ha! You wish."

The moment got slow as their eyes connected, sending a 220-amp electrical charge running through him. Crazy, that he would still be so affected by this woman. Surely, she felt it too. Yes, she did, he could see it in her eyes. And he also knew that it bothered her. He watched —half in fascination, half in frustration—as a veil came down over her eyes. She was retreating into herself. *The more things change, the more they stay the same.* He swallowed his disappointment, telling himself that it didn't matter. He was so over this woman.

Her brows knit together. "Why did you stop like that in the middle of the road?"

For a second he thought he hadn't heard her correctly, then saw the accusation in her eyes. An incredulous laugh broke from his throat. "Seriously? You rammed me in the back end and have the nerve to ask that?"

Just like that, it was on and they were back to where they'd left off —at each other's throats.

"It's your own stupid fault! You stopped smack dab in the middle of the road." She lifted her chin. "If I didn't know better, I'd think you did it on purpose because you knew it was me."

She was a piece of work, all high and mighty, snubbing her nose at the world.

His eyes narrowed. "What're you even doing here? Aren't you supposed to be in New York with your rich boyfriend?" He didn't try to hide the disgust in his voice.

She rocked back, her face draining. "H-how do you know about Parker?"

His gut twisted, wringing him out hard and dry. He'd do well to remember who he was dealing with here. "It doesn't matter what I know," he muttered. All he wanted to do was get this over with so he could get back to work.

She lifted her chin. "I came here to check on Bennie. She hurt her knee and I need to help her with a few other issues."

Alarm flashed over Dalton. "I just saw her a couple of days ago! Is she okay?" Even though he and Sierra weren't on good terms, he had a soft spot for Bennie. They'd grown close during the past six months that he lived next door. He wondered why Bennie hadn't come to him for help.

"I don't know. I just got into town and was headed to check on her."

Suddenly, Dalton realized the two of them were causing a spectacle in the middle of town. Shop owners had come out of their buildings, talking amongst themselves, their eyes lit with interest. In Sugar Pines, news traveled faster than a pent-up derby horse leaving the gate on race day. It wouldn't take long for word to get out that he and Sierra were spotted talking after their fender bender.

Phyllis Watson, his office assistant, came running out of Dalton's shop, her hands flailing. "I heard the crash, but was on a call with a prospective client and just now got off." She stopped in her tracks, eyes lassoing. "Sierra McCain?" In two steps she was at Sierra's side throwing her arms around her, squeezing her tight.

Dalton couldn't help but chuckle at how Sierra went stiff like she was being mauled by a bear.

Finally, Phyllis let Sierra go. "I haven't seen you in ages," she cooed. She put a finger to her chin, looking thoughtful. "Let's see, I believe it was right after high school graduation." She looked back and forth between Dalton and Sierra. The doe-eyed expression on her face was a stark contrast to the heavy innuendo in her voice. "The two of you were tight back then—couldn't wedge a sheet of paper between you."

Dalton cringed, then saw Sierra's face turn ghostly white like she wished she could crawl under the pavement. Blast Phyllis and her big mouth! While she was a good assistant and friend, she lived for gossip, devoured every scrap she could gather within fifty miles of Sugar Pines' city limits.

Phyllis gave Sierra a speculative look. "What're you doing back in this neck of the woods?"

"I came to check on Bennie. She fell and hurt her knee."

"Oh, I'm so sorry. I hadn't heard that." Her eyes danced as she lowered her voice and leaned in. "So, I hear you've got some high falutin' boyfriend in New York. Is he as good-looking as everybody keeps saying?"

Sierra shot Dalton a triumphant look. "Better. Parker owns one of the most successful advertising firms in Manhattan."

"That's so nice. You're sure lucky you got out of this po-dunk town and made something of yourself," she twanged.

The hair on Dalton's neck stood. "Don't you have some work to do, Phyllis?"

She laughed lightly, then shot him a sour look. "Yeah, yeah, boss. I'll get back to it in a minute. I'm on my break right now," she retorted, then leaned in and whispered to Sierra. "He's such a slave driver."

Dalton rolled his eyes. "I heard that. I'm standing right here."

Phyllis winked. "That was the point, sugar." She frowned, pointing to the accident. "Did the two of you ... hit?"

Dalton sighed heavily, feeling like he was pointing out the obvious. "Yes, Phyllis, Sierra plowed into the back of my truck."

Phyllis cackled like he'd said something hilarious. Then her eyes rounded. Her lips turned down, like she'd just thought of something. "Oh, wow," she mused. "That's ironic. Considering ..."

Sierra, flinched, her cheeks turning as red as her hair as she eyed Phyllis. "Considering what?"

"Um, your mother's accident," Phyllis stammered. She shook her head, her face draining. "I-I'm sorry. I shouldn't have brought that up."

Dalton wanted to shove a sock in Phyllis's insensitive mouth. "Then, why did you?" As ticked as he was at Sierra, he didn't want to see her humiliated.

Phyllis touched her hair. "Err ... it just came out. Sorry, I wasn't thinking." She forced a contrite smile.

Sierra straightened to her full height and glared at Dalton. "I'm all grown up now and don't need you to defend me. I can take care of myself."

He let out a hard laugh. "Seriously? After all we've been through together, that's all you have to say to me?"

Uncertainty settled into her eyes, and for a split second Dalton thought he might be getting through to her, but then her jaw hardened.

"If you hadn't stopped in the middle of the road, the accident never would've happened," Sierra flung back, eyes flashing.

He smirked. "You keep telling yourself that, darling. You had your cell phone shoved so far up your ear, a backhoe wouldn't have been able to dig it out."

"First of all, I'm not your darling."

Dalton leaned into her personal space. "You were distracted, and distracted drivers are dangerous."

"Whatever." Sierra shot him a blistering look. "You're such a moron."

Phyllis let out a deviant chuckle. "Sparks are flying, just like they always have between you two." She clucked her tongue. "Why don't you go ahead and kiss each other and get it over with?"

"What?" Sierra's jaw dropped. "I take offense to that."

"Take whatever you want." Phyllis shook her head. "But the truth's the truth." She looked at Dalton. "Anyway, I just came out to tell you that I called Eddie, and he's on his way over. He said it would take him a little while to get here because he was up a ladder, trying to get Mrs. Bigsby's cat out of a tree."

"Eddie?" Sierra asked dubiously. "Are you talking about jug-head Eddie who could chug a beer in one gulp?"

"No one's called him that in years," Phyllis said, the corners of her jaw twitching.

Sierra shrugged. "I meant no offense. That's just how I remember him."

"Eddie's a deputy," she said proudly, holding up her left hand to display a ring.

Sierra's eyes grew large. "Eddie Whitehead's a police officer?"

"Yep," Phyllis said. "He's thinking about running for sheriff next year when Luke Rutherford retires."

Sierra chuckled. "The Eddie I knew was always on the other side of the law."

"That was a lifetime ago," Phyllis snipped, giving her a cool look. "Lots of things have changed since you've been gone." She straightened her blouse. "If you'll excuse me, I've got work to do. Good to see you again," she said curtly, sauntering back to the shop.

Sierra sighed heavily. "I just shoved my foot in my mouth." Her eyes sparked. "But Phyllis deserved it for that crack about my mother." She let out a long sigh. "Still, the minute I get to town, I have a wreck and start insulting people." *Great.* "I'm batting a thousand here."

He gave her a sideways look. "You do have a knack for stirring up trouble."

"Especially when you're around."

For a split second, he thought she was attacking him again, then caught the wistful expression in her eyes that was gone before her next blink. A pang shot through him as myriad memories flooded his mind—the two of them skipping school and hopping in his Camaro, driving full speed with the windows down and music blasting to Huntington Island State Park. They'd climbed to the top of the lighthouse and looked out over the sandy beach that opened to the endless expanse of ocean. Afterwards, they went down to the beach and made a bonfire, snuggling close.

It was there, beside that cozy fire that Dalton first said out loud that he was in love with Sierra. She admitted feeling the same way. Dalton believed their love was strong enough to withstand anything that came at them. How wrong he'd been. A few short months later, it all came crashing down like a sand castle swept out by the tide. Sierra left for New York two months after he joined the Marines. From that point on, she cut off all contact. No explanation. Nothing.

Several years passed with him vowing to forget her. When he finally mustered the nerve to look her up, he learned she was practically engaged to some hotshot advertising executive in Manhattan.

She was so close. All he had to do was reach out and touch her face, run his hand along the curve of her jaw. Thread his fingers through those tresses of red. He jerked slightly reining in his renegade thoughts. The smart thing was to let the past remain where it belonged.

"Don't worry about Phyllis," he began. "She's sensitive when it comes to Eddie, works hard to keep him on the straight and narrow. Wants her fiancé to come across as a pillar of the community." He couldn't stop a grin from tugging at the corner of his mouth. "By the way, Eddie can still chug a beer in a single gulp."

Sierra rewarded him with an appreciative smile that shot straight into the center of his heart. "Good to know some things never change."

His eyes held hers. "Yeah, I guess," he said softly. There was still something between them, as alive as it ever was, whether or not Sierra admitted it.

She blinked a couple of times and stepped back, breaking the spell.

A stilted silence settled between them. He jutted his thumb. "I've gotta grab some paperwork from my office. Would you like to come in and wait for Eddie in the reception area?"

Her voice grew polite, like they were strangers. "Thanks, but I think I'll wait out here. I need to make a phone call."

To her boyfriend, no doubt. The feeling of loss that swept over Dalton was tangible enough to taste. He forced a smile, keeping his voice light. "Alrighty, then. I'll come back out when Eddie gets here."

She nodded.

He was a couple of feet away from her when she spoke.

"Dalton?"

He turned. "Yeah?"

"Good to see you."

The comment jolted him, confused him a little. "Good to see you too." He flashed his trademark apathetic smile, then winked. "Welcome home, Sie."

CHAPTER 4

*U*nfortunately, Sierra's rental car wasn't drivable, so she had to get a replacement from Pete's Auto Sales, the only company in Sugar Pines that rented vehicles. And as it turned out, all Pete had available was an old mini-van that smelled like stale French fries. Driving this decrepit vehicle around Sugar Pines was a little too reminiscent of how Sierra grew up. Maybe fate was punishing her for trying to rise above her upbringing. She let out a humorless laugh. She was certainly being punished for something.

Of all the people to rear end, why did it have to be Dalton? The irony was, if she hadn't been so shocked at seeing Dalton's last name on the sign above his office, she wouldn't have hit him. Seeing Dalton again had thrown Sierra into a tailspin. She didn't want her old feelings unearthed. Didn't want to question whether she'd made the right decision, fleeing to New York. Her mind kept replaying the fierce look in Dalton's silver-gray eyes and his easy smile. She didn't want to dwell on the unexpected flame of desire in her stomach when he'd approached her car. Or how her heart did a little flip when their eyes connected.

Crap! Crap! Crap! She couldn't do this. It was imperative that she stay focused on the goal. She'd always had a weakness for Dalton. He

29

was her kryptonite. Heck, half the female population of Sugar Pines probably felt the same way. Dalton was the epitome of attractive with his rugged looks and fearless take on life. She didn't remember him being as ripped in the old days as he was now. Heat flamed up her neck just thinking about the way his t-shirt formed to his defined torso and flat abs. Not to mention his cut biceps.

Sierra turned on the air conditioner, but it only blew warm, stale air. *Great!* She rolled down the driver's side window. Holding onto the steering wheel with one hand, she used her other to fan her face. It was ridiculous how worked up she was getting over Dalton. She felt freaked out and guilty that she'd had such a strong reaction to Dalton, especially when she was so totally and completely in love with Parker.

She tried to picture the compassionate look in Parker's deep-brown eyes. How sophisticated he was—knowing the best items to order on any given menu at the most exclusive restaurants in Manhattan. Parker was a whiz in the advertising world, known for his uncanny ability to recognize trends. He had the remarkable combination of being both creative and sensible when it came to business.

Parker was refined, graceful even. Whereas, Dalton was a blunt instrument—a fierce warrior who rushed into danger without a second thought. She'd loved that about Dalton when she was a silly teenager. But Dalton had his own share of demons ... demons that would ensnare her if she let them.

What Sierra wanted more than anything was stability. Something she could count on. She wanted Parker. Mentally, she started running through the list of Parker's qualities. She'd do it a thousand times, if necessary. Anything to crowd out these irrational thoughts of Dalton.

Sierra turned into Magnolia Grove where the twin mansions were located—Bennie's and the Drexel's. She scowled, still finding it hard to believe that Dalton had bought the Drexel Mansion. It must've cost a fortune. How could he afford it? He was probably getting some sort of retirement from the Marines. And then there was his construction business. But even those two combined wouldn't be all that much, would it? Maybe he was doing super well with his construction business. They were close enough to Charleston and Hilton Head for him to pick up business there.

Sierra didn't like the idea of Dalton being right next door, a mere football field's length away from Bennie's mansion. It was hard enough to put him out of her mind as it was. Having him right next door wouldn't help matters.

Her gaze trailed along the neat rows of burly magnolia trees lining the road on both sides. The blooms were at their peak, stunning pops of white amidst the vivid green, waxy leaves. Sierra rolled down her window and caught a whiff of the sweet-floral fragrance, taking her back to when she was a little girl.

Town legend had it that the trees were planted to represent the number of suitors the original Drexel Mansion owner's daughter Louise went through before finally settling down with her husband. There had to be at least thirty trees, if not more. Louise must've been a rounder. Sierra shook her head, laughing at the thought. The stories probably weren't even true. Or if there was a shred of truth, it was blown way out of proportion. No one could have that many suitors.

Before it was dubbed the Drexel Mansion, the monstrous mansion next door to Bennie's had been called the Radcliffe Mansion. Barton Radcliffe, a steel tycoon, moved to Sugar Pines in the early 1900s from San Francisco. He built the mansion for his new bride. They had one daughter named Louise. Louise was the belle of the town, suitors coming from near and far to try and win her hand.

When she finally accepted a hand in marriage and settled down, Barton built Louise and her new husband a mansion right next door. But Louise's husband turned out to be a scoundrel who loved to gamble almost as much as he loved fraternizing with the women. He put the mansion up in a poker game and lost it to Henry McCain. Henry had two daughters Bennie and Claire, Sierra's mother.

Henry McCain owned the mansion free and clear and had left it to both his daughters. When Sierra's mother passed, the ownership passed to Bennie who'd never married. It was understood that Bennie would leave the mansion to Sierra.

She couldn't believe Bennie had been stupid enough to take out a loan to fund an outdoor theater. The woman was completely losing it. And now it fell to Sierra to try to clean up the mess and save the mansion. She tightened her grip on the steering wheel, a wave of panic overtaking her. How in the heck was she supposed to raise enough money for the back payments?

Sierra turned into the driveway that ran beside the house. In the mellow light of the afternoon sun, the mansion held a sense of grandeur, like the by-gone South from storybooks and movies where plantations dotted the countryside and cotton was king. True to its antebellum architecture, the mansion had two spacious balconies, one stacked over the other, spanning the width of the two-story structure. The gleaming white handrails and spindles were separated by eight massive square pillars. The three gables across the top added the crowning touch.

Had the siding been white, the house would've been a shoe-in for Twelve Oaks, the Wilkes's plantation in *Gone with the Wind*. But Sierra preferred the soft moss color that blended with the lush green of the surrounding landscape. Black shutters flanked the windows across the front, matching the stately door.

Live oaks towered over the house, their far-spread branches reminding Sierra of protective arms. Spanish moss hung over the branches, like someone had artfully draped it there. Her heart clutched. This was home—her anchor. Even though she'd moved to The Big Apple and was making her way in the world, knowing the mansion was here had been a comfort. Sierra couldn't imagine losing it. She wouldn't lose it!

As she pulled around the back to the circular parking lot, she was surprised to see several cars. Probably people in the play. She blew out a long breath as she got out of the van and pushed her purse strap over her shoulder. She'd hoped to be able to greet Bennie alone, on her own terms without a bunch of people around. But that wasn't likely to happen anytime soon. Bennie thrived on having lots of people around.

Sierra left her luggage in the car, deciding to get it out later. She glanced toward the hill in the distance and saw the top of a wood pavilion. The stupid outdoor theater! It was insane to think Bennie had taken out a loan to fund the blasted thing. Bennie was going to get an earful from her ... after she made sure Bennie's knee was okay.

She opened the back gate and walked along the brick walkway that meandered through Bennie's rose garden. Then she went up the steps and across the covered deck to the back door, leading to the kitchen. It seemed silly to knock so she went inside. "Hello," she called, glancing around.

No answer.

The kitchen was shabbier than Sierra remembered. The white cabinets had yellowed, the paint peeling in spots. The once-white grout on the tile floor was now gray. Throw rugs on the floor were dingy and ragged. Dirty dishes were piled high in the sink. The island was cluttered with piles of paperwork and the remains of sandwich materials—a loaf of bread, slices spilling out of the package. There were open containers of mayonnaise, mustard, and a near-empty bag of chips. A stack of disposable cups sat beside a clear plastic pitcher of red Kool-Aid. The air reeked of sour milk, and the garbage can in the corner was overflowing, fruit flies swarming over it. Sierra cringed. Bennie had never been one to keep things super tidy, but this was ridiculous. Then again, Bennie was probably doing the best she could, considering her injured knee.

As Sierra strode down the hall towards the living room, she heard voices. "Hello," she said again, stepping into the room. Bennie, along with Nadine Thompson, her neighbor from across the street were laughing and talking to a group of people—one lady and two men.

Bennie looked up from where she was reclining on the couch, her knee propped up on a mountain of pillows. Sierra took a quick assessment of her aunt. Her silver hair was styled, rounding on her shoulders. She was wearing makeup. Her bright blue eyes were a little watery but still lively beneath her glasses, and she was dressed in a stylish, green pantsuit. Sierra's first thought was that she was glad Bennie wasn't wearing some ridiculous costume.

Upon closer inspection, Bennie was a little pale. But overall, she looked much better than Sierra expected, which was a relief and irritation at the same time. Sierra had dropped everything and rushed here to help, but Bennie seemed to be taking everything in stride. Then again, Bennie was a good actress, used to putting on a good face. She'd probably wilt like a tulip thirsting for water when her friends left.

"Sierra," she beamed, her face radiating joy as she held out her hands.

Sierra hugged her, getting lost in the soft folds of Bennie's arms. She inhaled Bennie's familiar scent—baby powder and hairspray. Memories of her childhood wafted over her, and she thought of the monstrous cans of Aqua Net hairspray Bennie used to buy. *The bigger the better* was Bennie's philosophy.

Bennie held Sierra tight. "I'm so glad you're here," she breathed dramatically like Sierra was the prodigal daughter returning from a long, arduous journey. Finally, when Sierra pulled away, Bennie announced, "Everyone, this is my beautiful niece, Sierra." She flashed Sierra an adoring smile. "She came all the way from New York City to look after me."

It was sometimes hard to know when Bennie was being genuine or when she was putting on a show. Considering Bennie had a captive audience, it was probably the latter. Bennie's antics were sort of endearing, most of the time. But today, Sierra was worn out from traveling and frustrated about the wreck. Speaking of which, Dalton's truck didn't look nearly as bad as the rental car, and luckily, it was drivable.

A dull headache was spreading across Sierra's forehead and all she could think about was how she needed to get ready for the brainstorming session tomorrow for Pristine Pizza. An automatic smile fixed over her face as she turned to the people in the room eying her with interest. In Sugar Pines, people were keenly interested in the comings and goings of each other, and every other piddling detail. In New York City, people couldn't care less about what other people did.

Hellos went around the room as people shook Sierra's hand and introduced themselves. Nadine gave her a tight hug and whispered in her ear. "I'm so glad you're here. Bennie may not act like it, but she really does need your help."

Sierra nodded, feeling a little better. Growing up, Nadine had been a confidant to her. She could always count on Nadine to steer her in the right direction.

"Have a seat," Bennie said. "We were just discussing the play." She pointed to the small-boned man with black hair and olive-toned skin. "Landon is the director. His son Teddy is taking over playing Macbeth for Freddie Allen. The poor man's too sick to do anything but lay around the house. His croup turned into pneumonia."

Landon offered a slight smile that didn't quite reach his eyes.

"And Myra is taking over my part." Bennie pointed to the fifty-something-year-old woman with white-blonde, short, spiky hair and round glasses.

Myra smiled and nodded.

"It pains me to say this, but Myra's a superstar in the acting world and will knock this out of the park. I'm sure the audience will be thrilled she's taking my place."

Myra blushed a deep red and seemed to duck a little under the praise. "That's not true," she argued, but her protest was feeble, like she was only saying it so she wouldn't hurt Bennie's feelings. Sierra's first thought was that Myra seemed like the mousy, skittish type who'd be better off backstage. Then again, Sierra knew from being around Bennie and her friends that some of the best actors had personalities like wet noodles off the stage. Their empty vessels would come alive when filled with other personas. "I'm glad you're able to help out," Sierra said, mostly because she wasn't sure what else to say.

Bennie pointed to an empty chair. "Have a seat, and we'll fill you in on the particulars." Her eyes lit up, her voice bursting with excitement. "Sierra's an account executive at a fancy advertising agency in New York. She knows all about marketing."

The comment was an invisible wand that turned the expressions on Bennie's friends to ones of awe. Any other time, Sierra might've been amused at how Bennie was hamming it up, hitting the touch points to impress her friends. But all she wanted to do right now was get her things unpacked and talk to Bennie privately, so she could figure out how to fix this mess. Sierra rubbed a hand over her forehead as she flashed an apologetic smile. "If you don't mind, I'm kind of tired. It's been a long day."

"We'll make it short," Bennie said, her tone leaving no room for argument. "You need to know about the play, if you're going to help." She jutted out her chin, locking eyes with Sierra.

Irritation sparked through Sierra. Not what she wanted to hear right now. She cocked an eyebrow, tempted to lay into Bennie in front of her friends. Then she saw the flash of amusement in Bennie's eyes, followed by a look of reproof. Bennie could be a force to be reckoned with when she wanted to be. And it had been ingrained in Sierra to respect her elders, even if that elder was a little on the crazy side. So she did what any polite southern girl would do—held her tongue and sat down. She let out a heavy breath. "All right, I'm listening."

"The opening takes place two weeks from tomorrow," Bennie began, "on a Thursday, with performances following on Friday and Saturday. It'll run for two weeks, meaning there are six performances total."

Sierra nodded. Parker wouldn't like the idea of her staying here for four weeks, but it might be her only option. "How many tickets have you sold so far?" Her heart dropped a little when she saw a concerned look pass between Bennie and Landon.

He cleared his throat. "Our opening performance for Thursday night is sold out. We've sold a little more than forty percent of the tickets for Friday and Saturday."

Not great, but a good start, Sierra thought. "How much are tickets?"

"They run from fifteen dollars for seating on the grass to seventy-five dollars for the better seats," Bennie piped in. "Plus, we give a thirty percent discount for children and seniors."

Sierra looked around at the faces studying her. "How many people does the theater seat?"

"Eight hundred and fifty ... give or take," Landon answered. "If the demand warranted it, we could probably put more people on the grass, another hundred, maybe."

Sierra hadn't even seen the theater yet. She hoped it was nice, since it could potentially cost Bennie the mansion. She squelched the irritation that burned her chest. "Has anyone done an assessment of how much profit could be made per performance?"

The man sitting beside Landon held up his hand. "Not necessarily profit, but I have the numbers for the gross intake." He thumbed through his notebook, then cleared his throat. "If we can sell at least eighty percent of the tickets, we should bring in around twenty-four thousand per show."

Hope sprang in Sierra's breast. Six shows total at eighty percent capacity would bring in roughly one hundred and forty-four thousand. Bennie only needed twenty-two thousand to get caught up on the loan. Of course, the numbers the man was spouting off were gross, not net. But still, expenses couldn't be all that much. She cocked her head. "How much do the actors get paid?"

Everyone looked at each other in confusion.

"That's the beautiful part," Bennie inserted, her face practically glowing. "Everyone's a volunteer."

Sierra's eyes bugged. "Really?"

A smile filled Bennie's face. "Really."

Landon pressed his lips together with a determined nod. "Yep, we love donating our time and efforts to such a worthy cause." He looked at Bennie. "We try hard to keep operating costs low so we'll have enough left to fund future productions."

"And to help repay expenses Bennie incurred in building the theater," Nadine added, giving Sierra a meaningful look.

This was sounding better and better. There was hope of saving the mansion, if they filled the seats to at least eighty percent capacity. Sierra ticked through the list of known expenses—set design, marketing, electricity for the stage, costumes. She grimaced. "I'm sure the Shakespearean costumes cost a pretty penny."

"Yes, normally they would," Bennie agreed. "But we're borrowing them from a playhouse in Charleston." She waved a hand. "Of course, there are plenty of alterations that must be done, but that's why we got Tracy Whitmore involved."

"Tracy's a wonderful seamstress," Nadine said.

Sierra clasped her hands, leaning forward slightly. "It sounds like you have the costumes under control." Her brain ticked to the next item. "How are you generating sales?"

They gave her blank stares.

She sighed. "How are you selling tickets?"

Landon smiled. "Oh, we do a lot of it through word-of-mouth and through our website."

Sierra nodded. "Do you network with affiliates?"

More confused looks.

"People who get a commission off selling the tickets," Sierra explained. "There are lots of tourist companies in South Carolina, which I'm sure would be happy to network with you. People would love to come to a quaint coastal town to watch an outdoor production." She tilted her head thoughtfully. "Do you serve refreshments during the play? That would be another good source of revenue."

"We've thought about it." Bennie spread her hands in defeat. "But there are just so many other tasks that need completing that we haven't gotten around to it." Her voice dribbled off as nods went around the group.

"Who's the best caterer or restaurant in town?" Sierra asked.

"Ivie Jane Compton," Nadine said matter-of-factly. "Her restaurant's by far the most popular in Sugar Pines."

Sierra gasped like she'd been punched. A heat wave blasted through her as she looked at Bennie whose eyes had grown large. More had changed in Sugar Pines since she'd been gone than she realized. The Ivie Jane Sierra knew was a spoiled rich girl who couldn't boil water, much less cater an event or run a restaurant. Then again, people probably thought the same thing about her—that she couldn't make something of herself—which was a huge source of her frustration with Sugar Pines. And now she was judging Ivie Jane the same way. Her rational mind knew she should be over the thing with Ivie Jane by now, but her emotions had other ideas. It was crazy how fast

38

the hurt feelings emerged, a wound that would never fully heal. The mere thought of Ivie Jane Compton churned acid in her gut.

"Um, I think we should consider someone else, considering the circumstance," Bennie said.

Nadine nodded, her face going redder than her lipstick. "I—I'm sorry, I didn't think." She looked at Bennie. "Well, it just happened so long ago that I thought it was over and done with by now."

Some things would never be over and done with. Awkward situations like this were part of what prevented Sierra from coming home more often. In their younger years, Sierra and Ivie Jane had been inseparable, until that terrible day when everything changed. She looked around, realized everyone was staring at her. Sierra didn't care to see Ivie Jane Compton again, much less do business with her. But making a big deal about it would only make the situation a thousand times worse. If she had any hope of moving beyond the past, then maybe she should take the first step. "You know what? It's fine if you get Ivie Jane."

Bennie studied her closely. "Really?"

She pushed a strained smile over her lips. "Absolutely. It would be better to use a local vendor to generate support from the townsfolk of Sugar Pines. The reason I brought it up is because it would be good to hire Ivie Jane, or someone like her, to run a deluxe concession stand. Then we can pitch it to tourist companies in Charleston as a dinner and play combo."

Nadine brought her hands together. "That's a splendid idea."

Sierra gave Nadine a direct look. "Would you mind contacting Ivie Jane and see if we can work something out? The easiest way would be for Ivie Jane to pay us a commission on her proceeds ... maybe thirty percent."

"Sure, I'll be happy to do that," Nadine said eagerly. "What type of food are you thinking?"

"Appetizers, deli sandwiches, soups, some upscale desserts." Sierra waved a hand. "That's not really my department. Find out if Ivie Jane wants to do it and then ask her to submit a menu."

Something about the conversation earlier was nagging at Sierra.

Her mind went back to the worried look that passed between Bennie and Landon when she asked about the percentage of tickets they'd sold thus far. "We talked about what we'd bring in if we sold eighty percent of all tickets. On average, what is your typical sell rate for plays you've done in the past?"

There it was, that uncomfortable feeling that settled over the group.

Landon cleared his throat and looked at Bennie like he wasn't sure how to answer. "Um, we sold about thirty percent when we did Newsies."

Sierra's heart lurched. She should've known those numbers were too good to be true. Hot prickles covered her and then she went cold. She wanted to flee back to New York—go back to her stable, predictable life. What was she even doing here? Did she really have it in her to save the mansion? Losing it was unthinkable, but orchestrating a play was way out of her comfort zone.

No, she couldn't think this way. Marketing was her game. Given the right set of tools, Sierra was sure she could pack the seats. But they'd have to go outside of Sugar Pines to do it. "You said you've been selling the tickets through word of mouth and your website?"

"Yes," Landon said.

"Okay, we'll have to expand to reach our target. Let me see your website." She'd left her computer in the van with her luggage. She looked at Bennie. "Do you have a laptop?"

Bennie wrinkled her nose like Sierra had asked her something distasteful. "You know I don't, but the desktop's still in the library though."

That's right. Bennie only used computers when she absolutely had to. Sierra had forgotten that little tidbit. She'd been gone from Sugar Pines longer than she'd realized. "I'll just run out to the car and get my laptop. I mean, I could check it on my phone, but it'll be easier on the computer. I'll just need to know the name of your Internet account and get your password."

Bennie chuckled. "Yeah, about that. I don't have Internet."

Sierra's jaw dropped. "Excuse me?"

"I figured it's one extra expense that I don't need," Bennie said.

It was all Sierra could do not to burst out laughing at the absurdity of the situation. Bennie had put herself in hock to fund a stupid outdoor theater and didn't have Internet because she didn't want the expense. Who in the heck could even live without Internet these days? Her aunt, obviously.

Crapola! Sierra was planning on taking care of her agency work through the Internet. She had a lot to do to get ready for the meeting tomorrow morning. She'd have to use her phone as a hotspot, but that could be clunky, and it would use a ton of data. She sighed, feeling the weight of the world pressing on her. She threw up her hands, pinning Bennie with a look. "Is there any place in Sugar Pines that has Internet? Or is everyone here as behind the times as you?" The moment the words left Sierra's mouth, she knew she'd made a huge mistake as a stunned silence froze over the group. Normally, she made a point of thinking before blurting the first thing that came to her mind, but she was tired and not thinking straight from all the stress.

Nadine's jaw tightened as she gave Sierra a steely look. "What kind of half-baked question is that? I have Internet, which you're welcome to come over and use anytime you need it. And you'll be happy to know we traded in our outhouses for bathrooms ... our horses and buggies for cars."

Yikes! She'd stuck her foot so far down her throat this time that there was little hope of getting it out. Also, she'd offended the only person she was semi-friends with. "I'm sorry, I didn't mean that the way it sounded." She flashed an apologetic smile, which seemed to thaw some of the chill from the room. "It's been a rough day," she explained.

Bennie eyed her with concern. "What happened?"

"Nothing that needs to be discussed right now," Sierra said evasively, flashing a wan smile. Everything was coming to a head, as emotion lodged thick in her throat. She swallowed, pushing it away, as she turned to Nadine. "Thanks for offering to let me use your Internet." Hopefully, Nadine would accept her token of apology.

There was a frosty look in Nadine's eyes as she nodded curtly. "You're welcome."

A feeling of complete desperation settled like a dense fog over Sierra. She'd managed to alienate the entire room in a matter of minutes. At this rate, she was bound to offend the whole blasted town by the end of the day. Sierra had no intention of hanging out at Nadine's house, especially not now that there was friction between them. "I hate to be a burden on Nadine and Hal. Is there any place public? A coffee shop, maybe?"

"The library has Internet," Landon said.

"Oh, I think Judy's café has it too," the man beside Landon said.

Sierra searched her brain, trying to remember the man's name. She hated to ask him now and let him know she couldn't remember. She'd have to ask Bennie later.

"Clydedale's Pizza has it too," Bennie said.

When Sierra drove by it downtown, she'd made a mental note to go there while she was in town. Now she had a good excuse. "What's the name of your website?"

"Sugarpinestheater.com," Landon said. "Would you like for me to write it down for you?"

"No, I think I can remember that." She thought of something else. "What about the set design?" The set could eat away much of the profit, especially if it were too elaborate.

"I was overseeing the set design ..." Bennie frowned, motioning to her knee "... until this."

"Is there anyone else who can help?" Sierra asked.

They all had deer-in-the-headlights expressions as they looked at each other. Finally, Bennie shook her head remorsefully. "I don't think so. Everyone's pretty tied up with their responsibilities. I can still make phone calls to coordinate things." Hope shone in her eyes as she looked at Sierra. "Maybe you could help? I'd need you to meet with the set builder on site to make sure everything's going according to plan."

Sierra made a face. "Me? But I don't know the first thing about set design." She shook her head. "I don't know that I'll have time to do that and work on the marketing." Especially while trying to manage her job at same time.

She could feel disappointment from everyone in the room, as they sat as silently as stones, watching her. *Sheesh*. This was a tough crowd. She'd come here to help Bennie and save the mansion, not to get thrown into all this extra stuff.

"I'm here to help any way I can," Bennie said.

"Okay," Sierra said, knowing Bennie would keep on until she agreed.

Bennie smiled brightly. "Good. Hank Trenton was building the set, but then his wife got put on bed rest." She shook her head, the corners of her mouth turning down. "Poor Mandy. She's had a rough go of it this pregnancy. Anyway, we were fortunate to find another builder. He's coming over this evening for dinner. You'll have plenty of time to talk to him."

"What?" Sierra's face fell. The last thing she wanted to do was to entertain someone at dinner. And the kitchen was a freaking mess. Sierra would be mortified if anyone saw it, much less ate dinner there. It wasn't like Bennie could get up and around, which meant she'd be doing the lion's share of the cooking. "I don't think dinner tonight's a good idea," she began. She looked at Bennie, trying to convey silently all that she didn't want to say out loud with everyone here. "I was hoping the two of us could catch up."

"Don't worry. We will," Bennie said smoothly. She cocked her head. "Normally, I'd just reschedule with the builder."

"That's a good idea," Sierra inserted quickly.

Bennie pursed her lips. "But we're way behind schedule. This dinner has been planned for a couple of weeks, mainly because the set builder's so busy running his business that it was hard to find a time that worked for him."

This just kept getting better and better! Trying to navigate Bennie was as impossible as pinning Jell-O to the wall. "Who's the set builder?"

"Dalton Chandler's been kind enough to donate his time," Landon said.

Sierra coughed, clutching her throat. "W—what? Why'd you get him?" A noose had been placed around her neck the moment she drove into Sugar Pines, and it was getting tighter and tighter as the day wore on. "No!" she blurted. "You'll have to get someone else! I won't work with him." She squared her jaw, ready to field any argument anyone could put forth.

Bennie tugged at her blouse, giving Sierra a frustrated look. "Dalton's a great builder," she blustered. "We're lucky to have him." She arched an eyebrow. "Regardless of your personal feelings on the subject."

Heat blotched up Sierra's neck. "This has nothing to do with my personal feelings," she shot back. Then caught herself. She wouldn't get into a tit for tat with Bennie over Dalton. Forcing her voice to sound calm, she pushed out the first thing that came to her mind. "I'm sure Dalton does a great job." *There.* She'd defused the situation, told everyone what they wanted to hear.

Bennie brought her hands together. "Good. Then it's all settled."

No, it's not settled ... not by a long shot, Sierra's mind screamed. She wasn't about to work with Dalton on the set design.

No way. No how.

Was this some twisted game Bennie was playing to get her back together with Dalton? Surely not! Then again, she wouldn't put anything past Bennie. She walked to the beat of her own drum ... be it good or bad. Sierra had agreed to let Nadine ask Ivie Jane Compton to do the catering, but this was too much. She lifted her chin, eyeing them. "If you want to get Dalton to build the set, that's your prerogative. But you'll have to get someone other than me to work with him."

The air got sucked out of the room in a big whoosh, then everyone got these uncomfortable, constipated looks ... except for Bennie, who laughed lightly. "Oh, so you still do having feelings for Dalton."

Sierra jerked. "No, I do not," she huffed. *Sheesh.* Her stupid face was boiling hot.

Bennie wagged a finger, her eyes dancing with amusement as she put on a thick British accent. "Me thinks thou doth protest too loudly."

Nadine half-sniggered, then placed a hand over her mouth to stifle the sound.

This whole situation was ludicrous. Sierra squared her jaw. "I have a boyfriend in New York. An influential, handsome boyfriend. His name's Parker." She glared at Bennie and Nadine. "Contrary to what you think, any feelings I had for Dalton Chandler are long gone."

A faint amusement trickled into Bennie's eyes. "If that's actually true, then it won't be a problem for you to work with Dalton. Now will it?"

Bennie had thrown down the gauntlet. "Fine," she huffed. "I'll work with him." She gave Bennie a sharp look. "But don't get any crazy ideas about trying to fix me up with Dalton because it's not gonna happen."

"Oh, I wouldn't dream of it," Bennie said sweetly, then stopped. "You called Parker your boyfriend instead of your fiancé."

Hot needles pelted Sierra. She'd not even thought to tell Bennie that Parker hadn't proposed. She could feel all eyes zoned in on her like lasers, knew her face was flashing like a neon sign. "No, we're not engaged," she said nonchalantly. "We've got plenty of time." She cringed at the look of relief in Bennie's eyes.

Sierra's phone buzzed. She leaned over and fished it out of her purse, which was resting on the floor by her feet. "Excuse me, I need to take this." She flashed a saccharine smile. "It's Parker."

"Her influential, rich boyfriend," Bennie added, a note of irony in her voice.

"Yes, that's right," Sierra said firmly, daring Bennie to say otherwise. "If you'll excuse me." She stood and walked into the other room for privacy. "Hey, babe," she gushed loudly. "I've missed you so much." She tensed at Parker's surprised laugh.

"We just saw each other yesterday and spoke a couple of hours ago, but okay," Parker said. "I'll go with that. For what it's worth, I miss you too."

"I know. It feels like it has been forever," Sierra said dreamily, then shot a scathing glare towards the parlor. *Take that, Bennie!*

45

CHAPTER 5

$\mathcal{J}$t was hard to believe Sierra was back in town. Dalton reached in the fridge and grabbed a water bottle, downing it in a few swigs before tossing it into the trash. He wondered if Sierra would be at Bennie's house for dinner tonight or if she'd find a way to weasel out of it, the way she'd up and left town two months after he joined the Marines. The only reason he even knew Sierra had left was because he called and her phone was disconnected. Then he got in touch with Bennie and she told him that Sierra had moved to New York. Bennie gave him Sierra's new number, which he called and texted a few times, but no response. He even tried emailing her, but got nothing back.

Sure, things had been a little tense between him and Sierra before he went into the military, but they were working through it. Things were coming to a head with Dalton's dad. The old man's drinking had gotten out of control and Dalton was tired of being used as a punching bag. It was during that time he started fighting back, not only defending himself against his dad but fighting against society in general. Dalton was drinking too much, and Sierra feared he was following in his father's footsteps—something Sierra wouldn't tolerate considering her own mother was an alcoholic.

Dalton plopped down on the couch and propped his feet on the coffee table, turning on the TV to a game show. How could Sierra leave him like she did, without a single word? Maybe he should've demanded answers today. No, then she would know how much she'd hurt him. It was better to let her think he didn't care. She obviously didn't care. She had her rich boyfriend and posh life in New York. It was better to let sleeping dogs lie.

Maybe he should cancel dinner tonight. No, he couldn't do that to Bennie. With the play coming up in two weeks, Bennie was desperate for his help. Also, he wanted to find out about her knee. Dalton's mom had left when he was a baby, abandoning him and his dad. Dalton had no memory of his mom, but he suspected his dad had been madly in love with her, one reason he'd turned to the bottle. Or was alcohol the reason his mother left? It was hard to know which came first because Dalton didn't remember a time when his dad wasn't drinking.

Bennie was the closest thing to a mother that Dalton had, partly because he and Sierra had been inseparable growing up and Dalton spent a lot of time at her home. That was one of the reasons why Dalton purchased the Drexel mansion when it came available. It felt like home to be here next door to Bennie. And aside from all that, he'd told Sierra that he would purchase it one day, proving that he'd kept his promises even though she hadn't.

Work had gotten crazy this afternoon. The electrical work at the new construction project failed, the inspector saying it wasn't up to code. Now Dalton had to get the subcontractors back out to fix the problems. Setbacks were a normal part of the construction process. Normally, Dalton let it roll off his back; but today it had gotten to him —probably because he was on edge due to Sierra.

Luckily, the damage to his truck wasn't too bad. Sierra's rental car had taken the brunt of the impact. When Eddie showed up on the scene, he asked the usual police officer questions, one of which was, "At what point did you put on your brakes?"

"Brakes?" Sierra asked, her face draining, letting Dalton and Eddie know that she'd not hit her brakes. In addition to having to pay for the accident, Sierra also got a ticket. Eddie apologized for giving an old friend a ticket but explained that the law was the law. He told her she could avoid having it go on her insurance by taking an online driving course. Sierra explained that she didn't have auto insurance because she either walked or took the subway in New York.

What kind of person didn't even have auto insurance? Sierra lived in a different world. She was no longer the girl he'd fallen in love with. Then again, it had been seven years since he'd last seen her. Plenty of time for a person to change.

His phone rang. He fished it out of his pocket and saw the familiar number. "Hey, Janie."

"Hey, how was your day?"

"Crazy, busy. How about yours?"

"Good. I picked up a new job."

"Congratulations."

"Yeah, I'm excited. It'll give my business a big boost." She hesitated and then her voice grew rushed, like she was nervous. "Hey, the reason I'm calling is because I was wondering if you'd like to come over. I'm making fried chicken, mashed potatoes, and biscuits."

Dalton's mouth watered just thinking about it. "I wish I could," he said regretfully. "But I promised Bennie I'd have dinner with her tonight. We're going over plans for the set design of her play."

"Oh, yeah. I'd forgotten that you committed to that. It's too bad," she pouted. "Would you like for me to go with you?"

"No," he said a little too quickly. "I'd better go alone this time. Bennie hurt her knee, and I wanna make sure she's okay." He realized at that moment that a small part of him hoped Sierra would be there. Maybe he was a glutton for punishment, but he couldn't seem to help himself.

Her voice sounded hurt. "Okay." Then she brightened. "But you're coming to the party a week from Saturday, right?"

"Right," he said dully, a weight settling in his stomach. Janie was putting together a huge birthday bash for her dad.

She laughed. "You sound about as excited as a man going to the electric chair."

He frowned. "You know I'm not big on those events."

"I know, but it'll mean a lot to Daddy and me if you come."

"I'll be there, but I won't be happy about it," he grumbled.

She let out a wicked giggle. "The silent brooding type. Love it!" There was a slight pause. "Hey, I've got another call coming in. I'd better get it."

"No problem." He was ready to get off the phone anyway.

"I'll see you tomorrow for an early lunch."

"Okay, I'll meet you at Clydedale's."

She made a kissing sound into the phone. "Ciao."

"Ciao," he said mechanically, feeling like he was talking about a dog. He scratched his head, wondering again how it was that he'd started dating Janie when the two of them were so different. Oh, yeah, because she pursued him relentlessly and because it was better to have someone to go out with rather than sit home alone.

Other than Sierra, there had only been one other girl that Dalton had gotten serious with. He met Miranda in Seattle. She was the office manager at the construction company where he worked. Dalton and Miranda got along well. One thing led to another until eventually she wanted to get married. He thought he could do it, had hoped he could forget the past and commit wholly to someone else. But at the last minute, he couldn't. So, he came back to Sugar Pines and started over. It felt good to be home, and he was enjoying running his business.

With Sierra back, Dalton was glad he was dating someone because she'd know beyond a doubt that he'd officially gotten over her. If Sierra was there tonight, it would be a good thing. He could get closure on her and finally move on.

SIERRA FELT like she was on one of those shows where someone kept tossing her another thing to juggle. After her conversation with Parker, Sierra holed up in her old bedroom and used her phone as a hotspot to answer the thirty or so emails she'd received from her team members about the Pristine Pizza account in preparation for tomorrow's brainstorming session. She outlined some preliminary ideas for the marketing plan and sent them to everyone. The ideas were mediocre at best, but at least it was a start. It was hard to come up with ideas on the spot. Her brain needed time to mull it over. Hopefully, by tomorrow, her tired brain would be able to summon a few golden nuggets, because she had nothing now. She closed her computer, switching her brain to dinner.

Luckily, by the time Sierra got back downstairs Bennie's friends were gone. She breathed a sigh of relief. "Bennie," she called. She went through the rooms, and found Bennie sitting at the kitchen table, talking on the phone, her crutches leaning against the chair beside her.

The kitchen was still a mess, but at least someone had put away the sandwich items. Sierra pulled out a chair and sat down. Bennie talked for a couple more minutes, then ended the call with a smile.

"Hey."

"Hey," Sierra responded.

"Did you get your work done?"

Sierra cocked her head. "How'd you know that's what I was doing?" She looked at the crutches. "You didn't come up the stairs, did you?"

Bennie chuckled. "Heaven's no. I couldn't go up those stairs in this condition if my life depended on it. I asked Nadine to check on you. She told me."

Sierra had been so involved with her work that she hadn't realized Nadine was even there. "What time is Dalton coming?"

Bennie glanced at the clock on the wall. "In about two hours."

Yikes! She was about to jump into action until Bennie held up a hand. "I was hoping we could catch up."

Yes, Sierra was hoping so too and then she came home to all of Bennie's friends. "But the dinner—"

"I pulled some steaks out of the freezer and put potatoes in the oven."

Sierra glanced over, just now noticing the platter of steaks on the counter.

"We'll make a salad and garlic bread."

The surprised look on Sierra's face must've spoken volumes because Bennie laughed. "Yes, I do have enough sense to manage on my own when you're not here, dear."

Heat crept up Sierra's collar. Evidently, she didn't or Nadine wouldn't have called and Sierra wouldn't have had to leave New York to save the day, but she didn't want to point that out and rub Bennie's nose in it. "What's the prognosis on your knee?"

"A torn ligament."

"Will it require surgery?"

"Doctor Clarke thinks it'll heal on its own if I take it easy."

"That's a relief."

Sierra shook her head. "I'm glad you're okay. I still can't believe you climbed up a ladder."

"Well, somebody had to fix those blasted stage lights." Her eyes narrowed. "I would've been just fine, but I leaned over too far and lost my balance."

A shudder ran down Sierra's spine. "You're lucky you didn't break your neck. You know better than to pull a stunt like that ... especially at your age."

Bennie arched an eyebrow. "Careful," she warned.

"You're not a spring chicken anymore."

"I'm not Methuselah either," she countered, jutting out her chin, causing the loose skin underneath to jiggle.

Sierra leveled a stern look at Bennie. "What about the outdoor theater?"

She folded her arms over her chest. "We discussed this already over the phone."

"Yes, we did, but that doesn't mean we can't talk about it now." Sierra's body tensed as she balled her fists. "How could you overextend yourself like that?"

Bennie waved a hand. "It'll be all right." She smiled in dismissal.

"Now that you're here. The play will go great and I'll have more than enough money to get caught up."

The hair on the back of Sierra's neck stood. "You don't know that. What if something goes wrong? You could lose the mansion." Her voice caught. "Does this place not mean anything to you?"

Bennie blinked rapidly, touching her glasses. "Of course it does." She shot Sierra a hard look. "Don't forget I'm the one who's been here these last few years while you've been off gallivanting in New York."

She rocked back. "That's not fair. You know why I left. You even told me you thought it was a good idea."

"Yeah, I told you that you needed to find yourself. But I didn't think you'd just desert us all and start living another life."

"I didn't desert you, Bennie. We talk all the freaking time." Blood was pumping so furiously through Sierra's head it felt like it might explode.

"What about Dalton?"

She let out an incredulous laugh. "What business is that of yours?"

"Everything about you is my business," she said stiffly. "Don't forget who raised you."

Sierra drew in a breath, trying to gain control of her emotions. She and Bennie ripping each other to shreds wouldn't accomplish anything. Anytime Bennie got backed into a corner she'd pull the *look-who-raised-you* card. "I'm grateful to you Bennie, for everything you've done for me. I know it wasn't easy losing Mom the way we did, and then you had to step in." Her words came out flat, devoid of emotion.

Bennie chuckled. "I didn't say that because I was expecting gratitude. I said it to remind you that as far as I'm concerned, you're my daughter."

Unexpected tears welled in Sierra's eyes. She couldn't stop one from spilling over and dribbling down her cheek. Hurriedly she wiped it away.

"I just want you to be happy," Bennie said, a tender look in her eyes.

"I am happy," Sierra countered. "Very happy. Parker's a great guy—the catch of the century."

"Yes, he may be the perfect guy, but is he the right guy for you? There's a difference, you know."

"Of course he's the right guy for me," she shot back. "We've been dating for two years."

Bennie looked thoughtful. "What happened to the engagement?"

"We decided to wait a while, give it more time."

She arched an eyebrow. "Two years isn't long enough?"

Sierra chuckled darkly. "Evidently not enough for Parker." Oops, she probably shouldn't have said that out loud. The last thing she wanted was to give Bennie ammunition to use against her.

"I see. Interesting."

The comment hit too close to home, she flinched. Sierra didn't know what mind game Bennie was playing, but it wouldn't work.

"I know you've got your head set on trying to find a hero like those in the Jane Austen novels you spent your childhood pouring over." Before Sierra could protest, Bennie held up a hand. "Not saying that's a bad thing because I love immersing myself in a good book. But you have to know the difference between fact and fiction."

She scratched out a laugh. "Really? You're telling me this? The woman who parades around town in crazy costumes ..." she made air quotes with her fingers "... to get into character. I don't think you have any room to talk." She folded her arms over her chest, leveling a death-glare at Bennie.

"Well, at least I know the difference between fantasy and reality."

Sierra jerked, her mind racing to articulate a comeback, but none came.

Bennie let out a sigh. "Look, I'm not trying to beat you up."

"That's exactly what you're doing." She'd been ripped to shreds by various people in Sugar Pines from the moment she drove into town, and she was getting sick of it.

Bennie gave her a tender smile. "Life doesn't come wrapped up in a neat bow. And heroes rarely come riding in on a white horse to sweep you across an English countryside." She let out a heavy breath, her keen eyes assessing Sierra. "You know, when I agreed to let you go to Camp Wallakee, I thought it would be a good diversion from the accident." She shuddered. "No twelve-year-old should have to go through what you did."

Emotion clogged Sierra's throat as she thought about those dark times. Her mother Claire was driving drunk. She weaved into the oncoming lane and hit a car head-on. Claire was killed instantly, while the other driver was hospitalized and died a few days later. As fate would have it, the other woman killed was the mother of Ivie Jane Compton, Sierra's best friend.

From that moment on, Ivie Jane hated Sierra's guts. She persuaded all the other girls to turn against Sierra too.

Bennie interrupted her thoughts. "When I sent you to Camp Wallakee, I never dreamt that you'd come home fixated on some silly pact that would shape the rest of your life."

Really? Bennie was going there? After Sierra came home from camp, she'd made the mistake of telling Bennie about the Jane Austen Pact that she'd made with her new friends. Bennie had laughed until tears dripped from her eyes. "Honey, that's the biggest load of crap I've ever heard. You don't need some stiff-shirted Mr. Darcy sitting around sipping tea in a necktie, but a down-to-earth guy who loves you with all his heart. You're not a prim and proper girl. What makes you think you'd even like a guy like that? Or that he'd like you? You need someone you can relate with." Sierra could relate to Parker just fine. Maybe he was a little too consumed with the agency at times, but that would change when they got married … if he ever got around to proposing, that is.

"I don't want to fight with you," Bennie said.

Sierra barked out a laugh. "Well, you could've fooled me." She sucked in a breath, clutching her hands.

"I'm glad you're happy."

"What?" she spouted reflexively, then blinked a few times when the words sank in. "Really?" she gulped, studying Bennie to see if she was telling the truth.

Bennie nodded. "Really. And I *really* appreciate you dropping everything and coming here to help." Her eyes went misty. "It means the world."

Sierra swallowed the lump of emotion in her throat as she nodded.

They sat quietly for a minute or two, lost in their own thoughts until Bennie brought her hands together. "Okay!" She smiled brightly. "We'd better get busy. Dinner won't cook itself."

"No, it won't," Sierra agreed with a chuckle. No matter how much she and Bennie argued, Sierra couldn't deny that they loved each other. With Bennie, you wanted to wring her neck one minute and hug her the next.

It was okay that Bennie didn't understand Sierra's insistence about holding to the Jane Austen Pact. Harley her best friend and fellow Camp Wallakee member understood. Harley was going to Cambridge for her master's program and had met the perfect Englishman, her very own Mr. Darcy in Wyoming of all places, where Harley was from. Harley just met him, but it looked promising.

Of course, all wasn't perfect for Harley. She was home in Wyoming to spend time with her dad, who was dying of cancer. It had pierced Sierra's heart when Harley talked about her dad and how she couldn't imagine life without him.

Unfortunately, Sierra knew all too well the pain of losing a parent. Both parents, actually. Sierra's mother Claire became pregnant when she had a summer fling with a man passing through Sugar Pines. Claire never divulged his identity, and Sierra suspected he never even knew he had a daughter.

Her thoughts went back to her conversation with Harley. Sierra admitted how disappointed she was that Parker hadn't proposed and how it had thrown her into a tailspin. Surprisingly, both she and Harley had been forced to rush home at the same time to attend to dire problems. Sierra let out a long sigh. Despite the uphill battle, she knew everything would turn out well in the end. It had to! And when she and Harley ended up with their dream guys, people would have to eat their words. Speaking of eating, they really did need to get cracking if they were going to get everything done before Dalton arrived.

Dalton's coming to dinner. The thought sent tingles shooting through Sierra, despite her best effort to quell them. She had to remain calm and collected.

No matter what happened, she wouldn't let Dalton hound her into telling him why she'd left Sugar Pines. And she certainly wouldn't tell him why she'd left him.

CHAPTER 6

*S*ierra's heart jumped into her throat when the doorbell rang.
"Dalton's here," Bennie announced, unnecessarily.

She swallowed, hurriedly placing the last of the silverware on the table. She rubbed her sweaty palms on her jeans as she glanced around the kitchen. She'd cleaned it the best she could, and while it looked a thousand times better than it had this afternoon, it was still cluttered and shabby. At least the food was ready. Well, everything was ready except for the bread, which was baking in the oven—the fragrant smell of garlic wafting through the room.

Bennie cocked her head, amusement lighting her eyes. "Maybe you should get the door before you melt into a puddle of nerves."

Her head shot up. "I'm not nervous," she flung back, trying to slow the pounding of her traitorous heart. She lifted her chin and strode out of the kitchen, down the hall, and to the foyer. Just as she reached the door, the bell sounded again. For a split second, she stood frozen. She had the irrational thought that the minute she opened that door, her life would never be the same again. She laughed at the absurdity. It was just dinner. Sierra would muddle through it the best way she knew how, and that would be that.

She sucked in a deep breath and pasted on a regal expression as she flung open the door. Warmth darted over her as she stared into those distinguished silver-blue eyes, the color of rain. She'd been too overwhelmed with the accident to notice earlier, but the angles of his face were sharper than she remembered. There were faint creases around his eyes, a touch of wisdom over his brows that hadn't been there before. He was still as devastatingly handsome as always, oozing that good ol' boy charisma that he wore like a second coat of skin.

"You cut your hair," she blurted. *Oops.* She'd not meant to say that out loud.

He ran a hand over his hair, which was still longer in the back, but more tapered around the sides than it had been earlier today. "Thanks for noticing."

Her first impulse was to defend herself, say that just because she noticed he got a haircut didn't mean jack squat. But she clamped her mouth shut instead, knowing no matter what she said, Dalton would twist it to use as a prodding stick to tease her relentlessly. Well, the old Dalton would have. But the man in front of her was different—harder and more unyielding.

She glanced at his lips, remembering those reckless kisses that had stolen her heart, claiming her for all eternity. Heat crept up her neck. Blast these infernal thoughts! *Claiming her for all eternity? Really?* She was a blooming idiot! She noticed the hairline scar running along his jaw. Had it happened during his service in the Marines? For seven long years, she and Dalton had lived separate lives. They weren't the same people as before. She flinched realizing that he'd been watching her study him. Her eyes met his defiantly. "What?" she demanded.

A slow smile spread over his lips, showcasing his dimples. "I wasn't sure if you'd be here tonight, Sie."

How well she remembered the husky edge to his voice—the sound of her name on his tongue. His words held a hint of innuendo, like she'd spent the afternoon waiting on pins and needles for him to arrive. Her eyes narrowed slightly as she stepped back allowing him to enter. He stepped in, closing the door behind him. They stood for a second looking at each other, a lifetime of strangled memories crowding around them. It was on this very spot that the two of them had hugged and kissed that last day before Dalton left to join the Marines. They'd clung to each other for the very last time, tears staining their faces. Dalton assured Sierra that boot camp on Parris Island was a mere twenty miles away and they'd see each other on Family Day, the day before his graduation. "It's only thirteen weeks," Dalton kept repeating. "Once basic training is over, we'll get married."

Sierra had smiled through her tears agreeing to everything, knowing it was a lie. She was already preparing to leave for New York.

"Dinner smells good," Dalton said interrupting her thoughts. She realized with a start that he was studying her intently. She got the impression he somehow knew what she was thinking. A smile fixed over her face. "Thanks. Come on in." Before they walked out of the foyer, she thought of something else. "Hey, would you mind keeping the accident between us?" she asked quietly.

Amusement simmered in his eyes. "You're in Sugar Pines, darling. I'm sure the whole town's heard about it by now."

She lifted her chin. "Well, Bennie hasn't. And I'd like to keep it that way, if you don't mind."

He shrugged. "As you wish."

She flinched. Before Dalton had mustered courage to outright express his love, he'd quoted "As you wish," from *The Princess Bride*. She gave him a questioning look, but his expression remained bland. She rolled her eyes. *Whatever.*

He motioned. "After you."

Her skin tingled with awareness of him directly behind her as she led him to the kitchen. Like always, he consumed everything around them so that she was only aware of him. She tightened her fists, willing herself to get a grip. *Sheesh!* It wasn't like she'd been pining away for Dalton all these years. This visceral attraction thing was getting on her nerves. She was happy with her life, happy with Parker. Maybe this was coming on because she was worried about the future of the mansion and upset because Parker hadn't proposed. Yes, that had to be it.

When Dalton spotted Bennie sitting at the table, he went to her side and leaned over, giving her a tight hug. "Hey, Ben," he said affectionately. "Smells almost as amazing as you look."

Bennie swatted his shoulder. "Oh, stop. None of that," she protested, but her eyes danced with appreciation as if devouring every word. She motioned. "Have a seat. We're just waiting on the bread."

Dalton looked at the table. "Where would you like for me to sit?"

"Wherever you want," Bennie said, waving an arm at the two remaining place settings.

Dalton pulled out the closest chair and sat down. Concern sounded in his voice as he looked at Bennie's knee. "I didn't realize that you'd gotten hurt. What happened?"

She chuckled lightly. "Oh, I did something stupid."

Sierra rolled her eyes, crossing her arms over her chest. When had Bennie not done something stupid? "Yeah, she decided to climb up a ladder and fiddle with the stage lights," she retorted.

Dalton laughed in surprise. "Bennie, you know better than that. You should've let me know, and I would've helped you."

Bennie flashed an appreciative smile that bordered on adoration as she touched Dalton's arm. "You're always so good to me, but I didn't want to pull you away from your business. I know how busy you are."

"I have been covered up," Dalton admitted. "But never too busy to help a friend."

Was it her imagination or was there a hint of accusation in his phrase? A reminder that she'd deserted everyone. Then again, maybe she was being overly sensitive. Sierra didn't realize that Dalton and Bennie were so close. Bennie had always been fond of Dalton, but they never really had a relationship outside of Sierra. Watching them interact made her feel left out, which was stupid. Why did she care what went on between Dalton and Bennie ... or anyone else in Sugar Pines, for that matter? Once they earned enough money to cover Bennie's back payments, she'd be out of here. Of course, she still had to make sure Bennie didn't get herself in a bind again. But surely she'd learned her lesson this time. Oh, how Sierra hoped that was the case.

Bennie looked at Sierra, a trace of amusement in her eyes. "Would you mind getting the bread out of the oven?"

"Sure." For a second, Sierra wondered why Bennie was looking at her that way. Then she realized that she'd just been standing there like a moron, staring at Dalton and Bennie. She hopped into action, glad to do something useful—something on which to channel these crazy thoughts and feelings. She slid the oven mitt over her hand and opened the door, removing the bread.

"Just place it in the center of the table," Bennie instructed, pointing at the trivet.

I know how to take care of bread, was the first thought that ran through Sierra's mind as she placed the bread on the table. But she only nodded. Then she removed the mitt and sat down.

Bennie held out her hands. "Let's say Grace."

Sierra's eyes widened momentarily. She'd not thought about it, but Bennie liked everyone to hold hands around the table during the prayer, meaning she'd be forced to hold Dalton's hand. She tried to recover quickly, but wasn't fast enough. Dalton's eyes narrowed a fraction as a corner of his lip tilted up in hard amusement. Her face flamed as she clutched Bennie's hand and thrust out her other hand. For a split second, Dalton just looked at her hand like he might refuse to take it. But then he touched her, sending an electric charge racing through her.

Bennie said the prayer, but Sierra barely heard a word. All she could think about was the feel of Dalton's skin on hers. His touch was light, like he was trying to maintain as little body contact with her as possible. For some reason this irritated her. She tightened her hold on his hand making such a strong connection that blood whooshed through her temples like a raging inferno. When the prayer was over, she opened her eyes to find Dalton eyeing her in amusement. She gave him a questioning look, then realized she was still holding his hand. In a flash, she snatched her hand away. Dalton let out a low chuckle. Bennie cleared her throat, like she too found the situation funny.

"I'll get the food," Sierra mumbled, standing to retrieve the platter of foil-covered steaks.

Dalton moved to stand. "I can help too."

"No," Sierra barked. When she saw Dalton and Bennie's surprised expressions, she forced a smile, her voice going buttery sweet. "I'll take care of it. After all, you're our guest." She placed the platter on the table, then reached for the potatoes and salad.

Bennie grunted, reaching for a slice of bread. "Guest? Dalton's more like family. How many times have the three of us sat around this very table?"

The last thing Sierra wanted was a trip down memory lane. To Dalton's credit, he only smiled as he turned to Bennie, changing the subject. "Tell me, what still needs to be done for the set design?"

Bennie placed a large steak on her plate and reached for a potato as she sighed. "Unfortunately, a lot. Poor Hank Trenton tried his best, but he's not nearly as adroit as you. And then he had to stop when Mandy got put on bed rest with her pregnancy." Bennie rambled on a mile a minute, listing everything that still needed to be done.

Sierra filled her plate with food, relieved to have attention diverted away from her. She made a point of avoiding eye contact with Dalton. Still, his presence was as all consuming as the sun. It took all the effort she could summon to remain distant and uninterested. From the corner of her eye, she managed to steal a few surreptitious glances. Dalton had changed his clothes from earlier to darker, dressier jeans and a short-sleeve, light blue shirt that picked up the color of his eyes. The fabric of his shirt stretched a little over his pecs and his tanned biceps rolled underneath his sleeves with every movement. Had Sierra only imagined the tattoo earlier? It was impossible to tell for sure because his sleeves were longer.

Her mind worked to fill in the gaps of the last seven years they'd been apart. Dalton served four years in the Marines before moving to Seattle, Washington for a couple years. When Bennie told Sierra that Dalton was getting serious with a girl there, the news hit Sierra like a punch in the gut. Then she stepped back and examined the situation, finally realizing it was good that Dalton was moving on. After all, she'd moved on. Why shouldn't he? Dalton deserved to be happy. Even though he wasn't right for Sierra that didn't mean he couldn't find someone to build a life with, as she had with Parker.

Something must've gone wrong with the other girl. Otherwise,

Dalton wouldn't have come back here. She was still wondering how he managed to purchase the Drexel Mansion. Looking at Dalton now, it was hard to believe he was the same angry, lost soul he'd been before. Dalton's intense hatred for his father fueled everything he did.

Sierra always figured the primary reason Dalton joined the military was so he could channel his anger into something constructive before it destroyed him. She always pictured Dalton drinking his life away, becoming an alcoholic like his father ... and Sierra's mother. Did Dalton drink anymore? There was a time when he and Sierra used alcohol as an escape mechanism from their problems. She'd been as much a party to that lifestyle as Dalton. But when Sierra moved to New York, she vowed not to touch another drop of liquor, and she hadn't.

There was a lapse in the conversation. Sierra realized with a jolt that they were both looking at her, waiting for her to speak. She put down her fork and tilted her head. "I'm sorry?"

"Bennie just told me that you and I are going to be working together on the set design." Dalton studied her, a quizzical look on his face, as he waited for her to explain.

"Yes," was all she said, heat creeping up her neck. Bennie looked relieved that she'd left it at that. Sierra could tell Dalton had a thousand questions, but Sierra wasn't about to air their dirty laundry in front of him.

"So you'll be staying in town for a few weeks?" he asked. There was a look of puzzlement on his face and something else she couldn't decipher.

She reached for her glass and took a gulp of water, then swallowed. "Yep." *Geez*. She felt like he could see right through her.

"What about your job?"

"My job?" His piercing eyes probed hers, sending all thoughts fleeing from her head, rendering her mind blanker than a new sheet of paper.

A tiny smile tugged at his lips, like he was enjoying watching her squirm. "A month is a long time to take off."

"You have no idea," she muttered, reaching for her glass to get more water. She took a long drink, then set it back down with a plunk. Her job was none of Dalton's business. "I've got it worked out," she said tersely.

"What exactly do you do?" His tone was musing, irritating.

"I work at an advertising agency. I was a junior account executive, but was just promoted right before I came here." She cringed. Why had she felt the need to tell him that?

Dalton offered a slight nod. "Congratulations."

For a second, she thought he was making fun of her then realized he was sincere. Their eyes locked and she caught a trace of something in them—regret, sadness, genuine happiness for her? Maybe it was a combination of all three. She was surprised that he was wishing her well. "Thanks," she uttered. An unexpected feeling of guilt splattered over her. Guilt that she'd left him without a word. Guilt that she'd not reached out to him in all these years. Guilt that she was giving him the cold shoulder now.

"Sierra has worked very hard to get where she is," Bennie added. "I'm really proud of her."

Sierra blinked a couple of times as she swallowed. Moisture collected in her eyes. It was rare that Bennie gave out genuine compliments, but Sierra could tell she meant every word.

Dalton cut off a section of steak and placed it in his mouth. He chewed a few rounds and swallowed. "Tell me exactly what it is that you do … in layman's terms."

"I manage a team of designers. We work with clients to develop advertising campaigns—media, print—it runs the gamut. I'm helping a national food chain now."

He cocked his head. "Oh? Which one?"

Briefly, Sierra wondered if she should tell him. Then again, it wasn't like it was confidential. "Pristine Pizza."

Dalton's eyes widened. "Really? The Pristine Pizza chain that's all over the nation?"

"Yep," she said, feeling a burst of pride. It felt good to be acknowledged for her work.

He broke into a smile that warmed her insides. "That's fantastic." His eyes held hers. "I'm proud of you, Sie."

Emotion lodged in her throat. Quickly, she looked down at her plate to break the connection. Where had that come from? As unobtrusively as she could, she took in a breath, trying to compose herself. It was ridiculous how out-of-control her emotions were right now. She'd always tried to picture how it would be if she ever saw Dalton again. But she'd assumed that she and he would both be married to other people. Being here in this house, where they'd spent so much time together was hard. She didn't know how to keep doing it. She moved to stand, but he placed a hand over hers.

Another zing went through her as she shot him a questioning look.

"I know this is hard," he said, as if reading her thoughts. Dalton had always had the uncanny ability to know what she was thinking. He gave her a slight smile. "But we'll get through it. Okay?" He motioned with his head. "Please, for Bennie's sake."

She nodded, removing her hand from underneath his. Somehow, she managed to pull herself together so her voice sounded somewhat normal. "Tell me about your business."

He broke off a section of bread. "What do you want to know?"

"So, you build houses?" Duh, that came out sounding stupid. She might as well have asked ... *So, is the sky blue? And the trees are brown and green?*

"Yes, I do mostly new construction and a few large-scale remodels."

"Dalton's a fabulous builder," Bennie added, helping herself to another piece of bread.

Sierra pushed the salad around on her plate before taking another bite. Dalton had always liked building things. His dad was a carpenter by trade and was super talented. Sadly, he had a hard time holding down a job because of the alcohol. She wondered if Dalton's dad was still around. She made a mental note to ask Bennie later.

"It seems like you've done well for yourself," Sierra said.

Long pause and then, "Thanks."

The word came out clipped and abrupt. *Sheesh*, this conversation was so stilted and awkward, like they were complete strangers. It turned her stomach. She was sure Dalton wanted to know why she'd left him without an explanation. Or maybe he didn't care. Maybe he'd not loved her as much as she thought. Maybe he was relieved to get away from her. Sierra looked down at her plate, an awkward silence filling the space between them. She had a lot of work to do before tomorrow's meeting with her team. Now would be a good time to excuse herself and go up to her room.

"Waffles," Dalton blurted.

At first, Sierra couldn't believe her ears. Then a laugh rumbled in her throat as she looked up, wide-eyed.

"I don't understand," Bennie said, shaking her head.

Sierra turned to Dalton. The corner of his lip was lifted in a crooked smile, amusement turning his eyes a dusty blue. A smile broke over her lips, dispelling the last of the tension. "Waffles, indeed."

Bennie frowned. "Would someone please tell me what is going on? You've totally lost me."

"*Waffles* is the code word Dalton and I used to say whenever we found ourselves in an awkward situation," Sierra explained.

Dalton placed his napkin beside his plate. "Yes, and I can't think of anything more painful than the two of us sitting here, awkwardly trying to make conversation, while pretending the past doesn't exist."

"Exactly," Sierra exhaled, a measure of relief settling over her. At least they were getting it out in the open. She gave Dalton an appreciative smile, which he acknowledged with a slight nod. For an instant, the years peeled away and they were kids again. A connection, as strong and ageless as the venerable mansion in which they sat, twined around them striking darts into the center of Sierra's heart. She got the feeling she'd fooled herself all these years. Perhaps she was as hopelessly in love with Dalton Chandler as she'd ever been. *No, no, no!* She had to fight against this. She had to remember what she'd worked so hard to build.

"Well, of course the past exists," Bennie began. She put a finger to her chin, looking thoughtful. "I can't remember which person said this, but our experiences shape who we are."

Sierra laughed. "Oh, no. Now you've done it ... got Bennie philoso-phizing. Thanks a lot. Now we'll be here all night. Next, she'll be quoting her favorite bit from Shakespeare about all the world being a stage."

Bennie's voice grew in volume as she began quoting, "'All the world's a stage, And all the men and women merely players; They have their exits and their entrances; And one man in his time plays many parts ...' From *As You Like it*," she finished.

Dalton burst out laughing, then gave Bennie a sheepish grin when she cut her eyes at him. "Sorry," he murmured. A look passed between him and Sierra as her insides warmed.

Bennie clucked her tongue. "Well, this takes me back—the two of you ganging up on me."

"I'm sorry," Sierra said contritely. She felt like a weight had been lifted off her chest. Suddenly, she was curious about his experiences over the past seven years—wanted to know more about the man he'd become. "Do you still play guitar and sing?"

Before he could answer, Bennie piped in. "Oh, yes. Dalton's a local celebrity. People always ask him to perform at events."

"Really?" Sierra cocked her head as she turned to him, relishing the color that crept into his cheeks. It made him look boyishly adorable. Dalton had an amazing voice and taught himself to play the guitar. "You overcame your stage fright?" She shook her head. "I never thought I'd see the day," she mused.

He shrugged. "I'm sure there are lots of things about me that you don't know."

"Such as?" She shouldn't have asked that, but she couldn't seem to help herself. Rather than answering, he just looked at her with pene-trating eyes that seemed to see into her soul. *Tell me about the drinking,* she wanted to scream. The Dalton sitting before her was nothing like the man she assumed he'd become. *Tell me that leaving you wasn't the biggest mistake of my life.* The space between them got inestimably small as they sat staring at each other.

Finally, Bennie cleared her throat. "I'm glad the two of you are getting along so well because it'll take a lot of collaboration to get the set done on time."

Panic trickled over Sierra and it must've shown on her face because Dalton waved a hand and said casually, "Don't worry, I can take care of the bulk of it by myself." He cocked an eyebrow, giving Sierra a challenging look. "I wouldn't wanna put you out or cause your boyfriend undue concern about us spending time together."

For some reason she couldn't explain, the comment made the hair on her neck rise as she straightened in her seat. "Parker"—she made a point of enunciating his name—"trusts me implicitly, as I do him. He has zero cause to be concerned about me and you working together."

Dalton smiled, a mocking laughter in his eyes. "If you say so."

So much for easing the tension. It was thick enough to cut.

Bennie smiled through the coldness. "Sierra, hon, would you get the pecan pie out of the icebox? I thought we'd have that with some ice cream."

"In a minute," she grumbled, turning back to Dalton. "I'll work with you any day or any time, and it doesn't cause me one iota's worth of stress. Whatever happened between us is ancient history. You got that?"

A hard smile slid over his lips, turning his eyes to balls of ice. "Yep, loud and clear."

CHAPTER 7

$\mathcal{N}$o doubt, Sierra McCain was the most frustrating woman Dalton had ever met. He couldn't believe she had the audacity to call him out like that at dinner. *"Parker trusts me implicitly,"* he mimicked. He barked out a humorless laugh as he pulled off his shirt and tossed it in the nearby laundry basket. "Well, Parker, if you really do trust your heart to Sierra McCain then you're a fool. Because she'll stomp it to bits and then flush it down the toilet without a second thought."

Even though he'd never met him, he hated Parker Henley. Hated that he was sophisticated and refined—the epitome of the Jane Austen hero Sierra had always wanted. The summer she went away to that stupid girls' camp was the longest of Dalton's life. He couldn't wait until the day she finally returned home. But then all she did was babble on about her new friends and the pact they'd made to find their own, true-life version of Mr. Darcy. Dalton didn't have a clue what Sierra was even talking about until he went home and looked it up on the Internet. He'd laughed out loud as he watched a clip of *Pride and Prejudice*. The men wore sissified clothes, and they stood so straight they looked like they had boards nailed to their backs. Their manner of speech was odd and stilted.

For months afterward, he teased Sierra, asking if she'd found Mr. Darcy yet. But deep down, he was ticked that she was trying to be something she wasn't. He assumed her infatuation would run its course, but then she started holding tea parties in the backyard of the mansion and making nasty cucumber sandwiches. Even though Sierra tried to act like they tasted good, Dalton could tell she hated them as much as he.

As the years went by, his and Sierra's friendship turned into something more intimate. Dalton forgot about the Jane Austen Pact, chalking it up as a fancy of childhood. It wasn't until Sierra took off to New York that he realized she'd never given up the idea of finding a more sophisticated man and lifestyle. Well, she'd certainly found it now. *Good riddance* was all he had to say about it.

He couldn't deny that a few times tonight, he and Sierra had a connection—the old flame reigniting like wildfire between them. No woman lit him on fire the way Sierra did. The problem was, it had always been Sierra. From the time they were kids, they were inseparable. He had no mother to speak of. His father showed only a mild interest in him when he was sober, and he was the devil when drunk. Sierra had formed Dalton's every thought. She'd been his home—his safe zone. Ironically, it was the drinking that initially brought them together … two children of alcoholic parents who didn't fit into the middle-class, well-adjusted family scenario that comprised most of the Sugar Pines population. That connection grew even stronger when Sierra's mother died in the car accident.

When the other kids turned their backs on Sierra, Dalton was there for her. He understood her shame, understood her pain. Dalton took it upon himself as if it were his own. He'd defended her to the nth degree. Had pledged his love to her. Never in a million years would he have ever thought she'd desert him. A piercing anger scorched through him, sending a streak of burning pain through his head. He wished she'd not come back. Things were going well. He was pretty much healed from the breakup with Miranda and was dating again. Now, his mind was a whirl, the past and present colliding in a big, dark cloud that would suck him in if he let it.

For the first time in years, he wanted a drink. The alcohol called to his blood like a siren to a sailor. He shook his head. No, he couldn't go there again … wouldn't go there again. He'd fought long and hard to get where he was, and he wasn't about to throw it all away.

Not for Sierra or anyone else!

He offered a silent prayer for help and felt a blessed peace settle over him. It was when he was in the military, stationed in Afghanistan, that Dalton developed a good relationship with God. He'd shared a room in the barracks with Randal Murphy from Lexington, Kentucky. The son of a preacher, Randy was always quoting scriptures and praying.

At first, Dalton had scoffed at this, saying it was a waste of time. He'd viewed religion as a crutch for the weak-minded. Dalton had never felt the power of God in his life. After all, where was God when he was growing up and left to fend for himself? Where was God when Sierra's mother was killed in the car accident that brought a mark of shame to Sierra and her family? It wasn't until Dalton reached a low point and realized that Sierra wasn't coming back that he started to feel differently about God. Prayer had literally saved his life, given him the strength to pick himself back up. The power of prayer transformed his life. He owed a lot to Randy. And while it was impossible to tell him all these things, Dalton could certainly live his life as a memorial to his friend.

He pulled back the covers and got into bed, pushing away the despondency. All in all, life was good. Business was booming, his investments were strong, and he was slowly turning this mansion into a showplace. He'd keep taking one step at a time, focusing on all the good things in his life. An image of Sierra's long, red hair flashed through his mind, crowding out all else. He saw her milky skin, the scatters of faint freckles dotted over her cute nose that turned up slightly on the end. Her full mouth, just right for kissing. The depth of emotion in her bright blue eyes, clearer than a tranquil pool of deep water on a cloudless day. Even after all these years, his skin still burned for her touch. But it was way more than just the physical. Sierra could finish his thoughts, almost before his mind could form

71

them. He loved her throaty laugh. Loved the crease that formed between her brows and the way she held her lips when she was deep in thought. Mostly, he loved the way he felt when they were together, like he didn't need anyone else in the world but her at his side.

He rumbled out a rueful laugh. Thoughts like this would do him in for sure. He banished all thoughts of Sierra as he turned off the light and closed his eyes, determined to get some sleep. Tomorrow would be better. It had to be!

~

"Is everything okay? You sound odd ... distant."

Sierra laughed lightly as she leaned back against the headboard, stretching out her legs. "Sorry. It's just been a long day." She stifled a yawn, weariness overtaking her. She had at least three hours of work but was so tired she could hardly see straight. Maybe it would be smarter to go to bed now and get up early in the morning when she was fresh. Parker interrupted her thoughts.

"Did you get everything worked out about the accident?"

"Yeah, I'm stuck driving a clunker, but everything should be fine. Thank goodness. The rental car insurance is covering everything."

"How's the person you hit?"

Her eyes rounded as she tightened her grip on her cell phone. "Okay, I guess," she said as nonchalantly as she could. Parker would freak if he knew that she'd rear-ended her ex-boyfriend. And that he'd come to dinner tonight ... that she'd be forced to spend time with him overseeing the set construction. No one could ruffle her feathers faster than Dalton. Ever since dinner, she'd been in a foul mood.

"Was the man hurt?"

She scowled. "No, unfortunately not. He's perfectly fine." She'd like to smack Dalton upside the head, wipe away that smug smirk on his handsome face.

"Excuse me?"

The shock in Parker's tone jerked her back to the conversation. She chuckled nervously. "I didn't mean that the way it sounded," she amended. Her mind scrambled to come up with an explanation to appease him. "The guy I ran into is an old friend from high school. He's super annoying."

"Is he giving you problems about the accident?"

She appreciated the note of concern in Parker's voice. "No, everything should be fine with the accident. It's pretty straightforward. Thank goodness neither of us got hurt. Dalton's just an all-around jerk on a personal level," she muttered.

Parker sighed in relief. "Good." He paused. "Dalton? Haven't I heard you mention him before?"

Hot needles pelted over her as her throat went impossibly thick. "No, I don't think so." She clutched her neck. *Crap!* Had she mentioned Dalton? Probably. She couldn't think of hardly a childhood memory that didn't have Dalton in it.

"He was your best friend, right? The one you used to go swimming with ... at the beach ... the times when you skipped school."

Why hadn't she learned to keep her big, fat mouth shut? For a split second, she thought about denying it, but that would only make Parker more suspicious. "Yes," she said simply, her voice sounding small in her own ears. She was surprised when she heard Parker chuckle. "What?" she demanded.

"So, of all people, you rear-ended your former friend?"

"Yep, pretty much." The irony settled over her, her mouth curving in a humorless smile. Fate was certainly having a heyday with this one.

"That's crazy."

"Oh, you have no idea," she muttered, pushing her hair out of her face.

"Wait a minute. This guy ... he's just a friend, right?"

Several things went through Sierra's mind at once. First, the term *friend* couldn't even begin to describe all the facets of her and Dalton's relationship. Second, Parker sounded jealous, which was kind of gratifying. "Of course he's just a friend," she heard herself say.

Parker let out a relieved laugh. "Good. How long do you think you'll have to be there?"

"What? Are my ears deceiving me? It sounds like the great Parker Henley might be missing me a little," she teased.

"Of course I miss you. On a personal level and business wise."

She rolled her eyes. With Parker, everything eventually went back to business.

His voice turned crisp. "How's the prep going for the meeting tomorrow?"

She rubbed a hand across her forehead. "I'll be ready, if that's what you're asking," she said dryly.

"Good. Don't let me down. We've got a lot riding on this. And I wouldn't want the office folks to think that your promotion is owed to anything other than your outstanding work."

It was crazy how fast the scorching heat rushed over her. "What?" she blustered. "I've worked my butt off to get where I am."

"I know you have," Parker said smoothly, "which is why I promoted you. I just want to make sure we don't drop the ball on this account."

She rolled her eyes, hurt settling like a brick in her stomach. "It's nice to know you have such little faith in me."

"I do have faith in you. I'm just worried about the circumstance. I hate that you had to leave so suddenly. This would all be so much easier if you were here with me. I miss you."

There was the slightest hint of vulnerability in his voice, which caused her to soften. She sighed. "I miss you too."

"How long do you think you'll be there?"

She chewed on her inner cheek, calculating the answer in her mind. It was still two weeks until the play started and then there would be two weeks of performances. At the very least, she'd be here a month. "I'm not sure yet," she hedged. Parker would lose it if she admitted the truth straight out. She'd have to find a way to break it to him gently. "I should probably let you go. I need to get some rest."

He hesitated like he might say more but then ended with, "Okay. I love you."

"I love you too," she said hurriedly as she ended the call. She tossed the phone down, where it bounced once on the bed. She hated this funky tension creeping up between her and Parker. In New York, everything had been clear. Her life was laid out before her in a straight and glorious path with all her goals nestled neatly at the end like a shining pot of gold. And now? She shook her head. Now, she was exhausted and not thinking clearly. Whenever Dalton entered the picture, things got complicated.

The essence of Dalton washed over her as she glanced at her bedroom window, the black square of night staring back, mocking her. *Now that you've come back, sat in the same room with Dalton, you won't have the strength to leave him again.* It had nearly killed Sierra to leave him before. The only reason she could do it was because he was away in the Marines. An image flashed in her mind—Dalton's lopsided smile that deepened his dimples. Few people realized how often Dalton hid behind a surly smile when he was frustrated or angry. But his eyes always gave him away. In the old days, all she had to do was look into them to discern what he was thinking.

Tonight, his emotions had run the gamut—hope, frustration, anger, pain. She balled her fist, pushing aside these treacherous thoughts. No wonder she didn't like coming back to the quiet and still of this mansion. It gave her too much time to think. In the hustle and bustle of the city, she never had to think all that much.

She stood and went to the window. Pushing aside the sheer curtain, she looked past the shadowy figures of the large oaks to the Drexel mansion beyond. From what she could tell, all lights were off. It was strange to think of Dalton living alone in that huge mansion. Then again, Bennie lived here by herself. But Bennie had always lived here because she inherited it. Not because she chose it. Her gaze went up to the pale moon casting thin shafts of light over the yard. Pops of intermittent light broke the solidarity of the darkness—lightning bugs.

An overwhelming feeling of nostalgia rolled over her, making her long to be out in that yard, dancing in the moonlight. She tugged at the window to lift it. In the past, it had raised effortlessly due to the amount of times she and Dalton went in and out it. But after years of inactivity, the wood was swollen. She grunted, exerting all her might. Finally, with an irritated screech-groan, the window lifted.

Sierra leaned forward, inhaling the balmy air, thick with the sweet perfume of magnolia trees. Her tongue caught the slightest tingle of salt from the ocean, less than twenty miles away. A warm breeze flowed in, bringing with it a slew of long-forgotten memories that whispered of home. It seeped through her pores and into her bones as she let herself get lost in the rhythmic song of the katydids and tree frogs. Despite the turmoil that Bennie had thrown them into, there was a certain comfort that came from being here in this house, looking out at the same scenery that her eyes had beheld since birth.

Her thoughts returned to Dalton, like water seeking the lowest course.

Dalton had always said that when they grew up he was going to buy The Drexel Mansion for him and Sierra so they could live next door to Bennie. Sierra didn't really believe it, but rather, it was a fantasy they could escape into when things around them got increasingly unbearable. A pang shot through her heart, bringing unexpected moisture to her eyes. She chuckled out a laugh. She'd been here only a few hours and already her defensive wall was crumbling.

She forced her mind away from the despondent thoughts as she moved away from the window. The breeze coming in pushed out the stuffiness, restoring a measure of calm as she sat down on the bed and opened her laptop. While on the phone with Parker, she felt like she could sink into the bed and sleep for days. But now, sleep had fled.

She might as well get a little work done. It would help occupy her mind, keep her from thinking about the one man she shouldn't. Even as the phrase ran through her mind, another image of Dalton flashed before her eyes.

Stop it, she commanded herself, squelching the thought. "Okay, Pristine Pizza," she said aloud. "Let's see what kick-butt marketing plan I can design for you."

CHAPTER 8

"*H*urry up, Sie! Don't be such a slow poke."

"I'm coming," Sierra grumbled, but a smile stole over her lips as she looked at the excitement dancing in Dalton's eyes. It fascinated Sierra how his eye color changed with his emotions. Today, they were more blue than silver. When they were younger, Dalton was gangly and awkward, but overnight, he'd transformed into a hunk. And he seemed to be growing more handsome with each passing day. Girls at school had noticed it too, which Sierra wasn't happy about. But thankfully, Dalton only seemed to have eyes for her. Her breath came out in short bursts with each step as she gripped the handrail. "How many steps are there in this wretched lighthouse anyway? A gazillion?"

"One hundred and sixty-seven."

She wrinkled her nose. "It feels like a heck of a lot more than that."

He glanced back over his shoulder. "That's because the staircase is curved."

"Oh, yeah. I hadn't noticed," she mumbled. Dalton was fascinated with architecture and knew every detail about this lighthouse, including how it was constructed of cast iron plates in case it needed to be relocated. It had, in fact, been relocated in the late 1800s due to erosion—a mile and a quarter back from the shore. Sierra remembered Dalton rambling off that fact the last time they'd come.

When Sierra finally reached the top, she stood, trying to catch her breath.

He grinned. "You made it. I was afraid I might have to carry you."

She rolled her eyes, giving him a playful nudge. "Yeah, yeah."

Dalton stepped up behind her and pulled her into his arms. Tingles circled down her spine when his lips nuzzled her ear. The wind whipped around them, flapping against their clothes as she snuggled into Dalton, appreciating the warmth of his body. His arms felt strong and secure around her. "It's nice to have the lighthouse all to ourselves. What do you think?" he murmured.

Her gaze swept over the green canopy of trees directly below, past the sandy beach, and out at the endless ocean, sparkling like glass in the afternoon sun. "It's incredible."

He turned her around to face him. "Yes, you are." His eyes roved over her in that leisurely way that sent all thoughts flying out of her head. He leaned closer, a fierce look flickering in his magnetic eyes. "No matter what happens from here on out, promise me that we'll always be together."

"I promise," she whispered.

His lips came down on hers, tantalizing and soft as a feather that tickled and teased. Just when she was craving more, he drew back. "You taste like Twizzlers."

A laugh escaped her throat. "So do you."

"I like it," he murmured, tightening his hold on her waist as his hands moved up her back. His lips came down on hers, sending a jolt of electricity buzzing through her. The kiss grew more demanding, sending a hot fire wicking through Sierra as she gave into the demands of his lips. Glorious rapture rolled inside her and all she could think about was Dalton—her everything. A groan rumbled in her throat as he buried his hands in her hair, dipping her back.

No, it was more of a moan. A loud series of moans or were they groans? Groans of pain, not pleasure. Sierra shot up in bed, her heart pounding erratically. She touched her lips, still feeling the burn from Dalton's kiss. For a split second, the loss of him was so overwhelming that it squeezed her heart like a vise. She flinched, embarrassment flooding over her as she threw back the covers. That stupid dream had been so real! She drew in a breath, trying to get a hold of herself. *Geez.* This attraction-thing was getting ridiculous!

She wadded the sheet in her fist and lay back against the pillow, memories from the dream wrapping around her like a cocoon. In her half-dream state, it was easy to let herself drift back into Dalton's arms. *Just for tonight,* she promised herself. She was almost back to sleep when she heard the moans. She tensed, her heart pounding as she sat up again. She cocked her ears. There it was again. *Bennie!*

She jumped out of bed and ran down the hall to Bennie's room. Without knocking, she flung open the door. Bennie was sitting in bed, clutching her knee, moaning in pain.

Sierra rushed to her side. "Are you okay?"

"My knee," Bennie screeched, her face pinched with pain.

A feeling of helplessness overtook Sierra. "What can I do to help? Do you need some pain medication?" She tried to think. "Should I call someone? Nadine? 911?"

Bennie rocked back and forth. "Call Dalton."

She jerked. "What?"

Bennie caught her arm in an iron grip. The whites of her eyes popping in panic. "I need you to call Dalton. Right now! Tell him ..." she gulped a breath, trying to get the words out "... I need him to take me ... to the Emergency Room." Tears streamed down her face as she moaned. "I'm sorry," she lamented. She drew in a labored breath. "Something's wrong."

"Okay." Sierra looked around wildly. "Where's your phone?"

"There." Bennie pointed to the dresser.

Sierra rushed over and grabbed it, but it was locked. "I need your passcode."

"5467."

She punched it in and typed Dalton's name in the search. Luckily, it came right up. She called. It rang a few times, then went to his voicemail. A cold sweat broke across Sierra's brow. "He's not answering. Maybe I should call 911."

Bennie gritted her teeth, wincing in pain. "No, try him again."

Sierra tried a couple more times, frustration welling inside her. "He's not answering." Tears sprang to her eyes. It hurt to see her aunt in such a state. Bennie was coiled up tight, holding her knee, still moaning. "I've got to get you some help."

"Run over and get Dalton."

An incredulous laugh broke through her throat. "What?"

"Now!" Bennie shouted, breaking into sobs. "I need him to take me to the Emergency Room."

"But 911's faster."

She shook her head. "Too expensive. I don't have good insurance."

Horror trickled down Sierra's spine. In all the years Sierra had been away, she'd not thought twice about what type of insurance Bennie had. Aside from the income from the plays, Bennie taught piano and voice lessons. Of course she didn't have good insurance. Sierra thought about the cushy policy she had through the ad agency, guilt slicing through her. "Okay," she heard herself say. "I'll go get him."

"Put something on first," Bennie barked.

Sierra pushed her hair out of her face. "What?" Then she looked down and realized she was only wearing a long t-shirt and underwear. "Oh, yeah." She touched Bennie's shoulder. "Will you be okay while I'm next door?"

Bennie bit down on her lower lip, nodding. In the semi-darkness, Bennie's face took on the look of a shriveled walnut, dented and bruised with age. Sierra's heart pounded out a sickly beat. She had to hurry. Had to get Bennie to the hospital, even if that meant dragging Dalton's butt out of bed.

She squared her jaw, resolve crowding out uncertainty as she jumped into action. "I'll be back soon," she yelled over her shoulder as she darted out of the room.

Please help Bennie, she prayed.

⁓

THE GRASS WAS wet under Sierra's feet as she ran across the yard. Not wanting to waste time putting on shoes, she'd thrown on a pair of shorts and darted out the door. She shrieked and nearly fell when a prickly burr dug into the ball of her foot. She stopped only long enough to remove it and kept going.

She punched Dalton's doorbell, trying to figure out what she'd do if he didn't answer. It then occurred to Sierra that she could drive Bennie to the emergency room. In all the commotion, she'd not thought about that. *Crap!* No, she couldn't. There was no way she could lift Bennie, which is why Bennie wanted Dalton.

She felt like a bedraggled fool standing out here in the middle of the night. What time was it anyway? Two or three in the morning? She jabbed the doorbell again and again, cursing under her breath. When that didn't yield results, she pounded on the door. "Dalton! Open up!"

Her panic was mounting to the point of frenzy as she continued knocking, frustrated tears pumping into her eyes. Finally, after what seemed like an eternity, she heard footsteps and then Dalton opened the door.

He looked, then looked again. "Sierra?" he said, like he was talking to himself. His hair was messy, a crease running along his cheek like he'd been sleeping hard. She noticed again the hairline scar, tracing the edge of his jaw.

She clutched her t-shirt. "Hey." Her eyes trailed to his chest as she realized he wasn't wearing a shirt. Wow! Sculpted pecs, flat abs carved from stone. Dalton had certainly not looked like this before. Heat blasted over her as she looked at his right bicep and saw that he did, indeed, have a tattoo—two thin, parallel bands circling the radius of his arm. Her eyes flickered over his red boxer shorts and long, muscular legs.

Maybe it was because of the dream she'd just had, but she felt again the intense desire she'd experienced earlier when his lips touched hers. Her pulse pounded like a rock band against her temples. She shook her head, clearing away the wretched thoughts. It was crazy how all of that could rush through her head in the blink of an eye, especially when she was worried sick about Bennie.

Dalton cocked his head in confusion, then frustration masked his features. "What're you doing here?" He looked her up and down, frowning in disapproval.

"It's Bennie," she stammered. "Her knee. She's in a lot of pain and needs you—us—to take her to the Emergency Room. I tried to call, but you didn't answer." The words spilled out and disappeared into the night air as she blinked rapidly to stay the emotion. Goosebumps rose over her flesh as she hugged her arms.

Concern washed over him as he nodded. He pushed a hand through his hair. "I must've accidentally put my phone on silent." He stepped back and motioned. "Come in while I get dressed."

"Hurry, she's in bad shape."

DALTON'S HEAD felt sluggish and too large for his body as he tried to fully wake up. When he first opened the door and saw Sierra standing on the steps, he thought he must be dreaming. But when she told him the bit about Bennie, he knew it was real. As they jogged side-by-side to Bennie's mansion, he glanced sideways at Sierra. Even though her face was tight with worry, she was still beautiful, her milky skin reflecting the moonlight, her long red hair flying out behind her like flames.

When they stepped inside the mansion, Dalton heard the groans. His heart dropped as he looked at Sierra. The look in her eyes reflected his own fears. This was bad!

They rushed down the hall to Bennie's room. For an instant, he stood paralyzed at the sight of Bennie rocking back and forth, her expression streaked with pain as she moaned. Sierra tugged on his arm.

"Come on," she urged, frustration lacing her voice. "I need you to help me get her up so we can take her to the hospital."

"Thanks for coming," Bennie managed to utter, then drew in a halting breath.

Dalton nodded. "I think I can carry her," he said to Sierra.

Sierra's eyes rounded. "Are you sure? It wouldn't be good to drop her."

"No, it wouldn't," Bennie said.

Dalton was surprised that Bennie had joined the conversation, considering her pain level. "No worries. I've got you, Bennie. Put your arm around my shoulders," he instructed as he lifted her. Bennie was still grimacing in pain—soft, intermittent moans issuing from her throat.

"Grab my crutches," Bennie said to Sierra. "And my purse."

Sierra nodded as she reached for the items. "Crap! I forgot. I'm driving that horrid van because of the accident."

"What accident?" Bennie asked, then groaned again.

"Never mind that," Sierra inserted quickly, looking at Dalton. "Maybe we should take your truck. Or your Camaro? Do you still have it?"

"Of course." He'd never get rid of the Camaro, but it was more of a collectible. Dalton tried to think. "I can put Bennie down on the couch and run and get the truck."

"No need," Bennie grunted. She squeezed her eyes shut, tears streaming down her cheeks. "Sorry," she breathed, wringing her hands. "It just hurts so badly." Dalton's stomach twisted, it was tough seeing Bennie this way. "We can take my car," Bennie managed to say.

As carefully as he could, Dalton put Bennie in the passenger seat and got behind the wheel. He looked in the rearview mirror at Sierra. "Which hospital?" There were three hospitals, all of them roughly twenty-five to thirty minutes away.

"St. Thomas," Bennie croaked.

"Really?" Dalton hadn't even thought about that one. It was a good fifty minutes away.

"That's where I want to go," Bennie said firmly, leaving no room for argument.

He looked at Sierra again, and she shrugged. "If that's where she wants to go."

He started the engine. "St. Thomas it is."

CHAPTER 9

When they arrived at St. Thomas, Dalton pulled along the curb next to the entrance. "I'll get Bennie inside, if you'll park the car," he said.

Sierra nodded. "Okay. Thanks," she added dully.

On the drive over, Bennie's pain subsided a little, and she'd slept. Meanwhile, Sierra and Dalton rode in silence. Sierra hated this wall between them, hated that she was so dang awkward around him. She regretted being too much of a coward to open up a conversation about why she'd left him and gone to New York.

Sierra rushed into the Emergency Room and glanced around the waiting room. It was empty. She stepped up to the window. "Hello, my aunt Bennie McCain was just brought in."

The lady nodded. "She was just taken back to a room." She pressed a button, opening the white double doors. "Go on back. Take the first immediate right, and you'll see her room."

"Thanks," Sierra said, hurrying through the doors. She spotted Bennie's room, saw Dalton sitting in a chair beside the bed. She rushed in, then stopped in her tracks when she saw a familiar face. "Hello," she mumbled. He was one of Bennie's friends who'd been at the mansion—the man whose name she couldn't remember.

He smiled in recognition. "Hi, Sierra."

"Hey." What was the guy's name? About Bennie's age, he was average build and height with dark hair, thinning on top. He was dressed in blue nursing scrubs with white tennis shoes.

She cocked her head. "You work here?"

"Yes, I'm a nurse." He turned his attention back to Bennie, giving her an affectionate smile. "I'm glad I was on call tonight. My shift was just ending when I saw Bennie come in."

Bennie's lips formed a thin line as she smiled slightly. "Me too, Wesley. One minute I was sound asleep, and the next, the pain hit." She shuddered. "It was terrible."

Wesley. Sierra committed the name to memory, taking an assessment of Bennie. She was still in pain, her face as white as the bedsheets. But at least she wasn't moaning. Wesley patted Bennie's hand. "You're gonna be okay. The doctor will be in soon. What's your pain level now?"

"About a four or five. It was through the roof," Bennie said. Her voice sounded weak and fatigued.

Dalton nodded, his mouth forming a grim line. "Yeah, it was bad."

"Yes, it was," Sierra agreed.

Wesley touched Bennie's shoulder. "Well, you're in good hands now, love. I asked one of the nurses to give you something to take the edge off. She'll be in soon."

"Thank you." Bennie smiled, her cheeks taking on some of their normal color. "I knew I could count on you."

For a split second, Bennie looked like her rosy, vibrant self. It struck Sierra then that there was more than just friendship between them. No wonder Bennie had been adamant about coming here. She and Wesley were an item, and Bennie had to know he was working tonight. Well, at least one thing had worked out well. Now if the nurse could give Bennie something to help ease the pain and the doctor could shed some light on why it hit so suddenly, they'd be in good shape.

Sierra stood there for a second, looking at the empty chair beside Dalton. She couldn't very well stand here like an idiot, but she didn't relish the idea of sitting next to him. *Sheesh.* Her cells would go into overdrive being that close. Bennie and Wesley were talking amongst themselves, but Dalton …. She realized he was watching her with an amused expression, like he knew how uncomfortable his presence made her. She lifted her chin and strode over to the chair beside him, ignoring the tingling sensation buzzing through her body.

Dalton was wearing the same jeans and shirt from dinner. His hair was messy, but overall, he looked good. Too bad Sierra couldn't say the same for herself. Her hair was stringy, and she didn't have on a speck of makeup. Her once-yellow t-shirt was faded to a bone color, and it swallowed her whole. She kept it because it was so comfortable to sleep in, never dreaming that she'd wear it out. If her roommate Juliette saw her now, she'd be appalled. Then again, Dalton was seeing her this way, which was a thousand times worse!

An incredulous laugh bubbled in Sierra's throat as she swallowed. Maybe she was still asleep and this was a nightmare. After all, the kiss had felt so real. Heat crept up her neck as she pulled at her collar.

"Are you okay?"

She flinched realizing Dalton was talking to her. "Me? I'm fine." She rolled her eyes like he was an idiot for asking.

His perceptive eyes flickered over her, a crooked smile tugging at the corner of his lip.

She ran a hand over her shirt. "What?"

He shook his head. "Nothing."

"Go ahead and say it." She gave him a dark look. "I look like crap."

An easy laugh escaped his throat. "Those are your words."

She scowled. "Well, you were thinking it," she said tartly.

He turned to face her, a perplexed expression on his handsome face. "Does everything have to be a fight with you?"

The question caught her off guard. "What?" *Dang it!* Why did he have to be so flipping attractive?

Frustration settled into his eyes, turning them slate gray. "Ever since we first saw each other yesterday, you've been fighting me at every turn."

Had she? It was on her tongue to deny it, but she knew it was true.

She'd gone on the offensive to deflect her attraction to him. Her shoulders sagged. "You're right," she said, surprised that she'd admitted it out loud. "I'm sorry."

His eyes widened in surprise. Then a smile stole over his lips, his dimples showing. It was the exact same expression he'd worn in her dream, the one that turned her insides to mush. "And contrary to what you said. You don't look like crap."

"I don't?" She blinked a couple of times.

He chuckled. "No, you look kind of cute."

The distance between them shrank as her heart pounded. Her eyes seemed to have a mind of their own as they locked with his. It would be so easy to kiss him right now, see if the real thing was as good as it had been in her dream.

"Well, except for that one tangle."

"Tangle?" she asked dubiously.

He touched her hair, energy pulsing through her. "Yeah, right here in the back."

Her stomach turned flips. "Thanks."

The doctor entered the room. Wesley stepped away from Bennie at the same time Sierra angled away from Dalton. *Geez.* She'd almost lost it there for a minute, right here in the ER. It was uncanny how much control Dalton wielded over her. No wonder she'd had to wait until he was at basic training before she escaped all those years ago. Not much had changed. Parker would be mortified if he knew she was having all these feelings for Dalton. He could never know. No one could!

The young doctor flashed a professional smile. "Hello, I'm Mike Givens the doctor in charge. I understand you're having some pain." He motioned to her knee. "Did you injure it tonight?"

Bennie's voice was feeble and strained as she answered. "No, I hurt it a few days ago when I fell from a ladder."

Mike winced. "Ouch."

"She has a torn ligament," Wesley explained. "Bennie's a close friend, so I decided to stick around after my shift to make sure she's okay."

Mike pursed his lips, nodding. Then he turned his attention back to Bennie. "What's your pain level now?"

"About a four. It spiked up to a twelve or thirteen, which is why I came in."

"I asked a nurse to get her something to take the edge off the pain," Wesley said.

Mike nodded. "Good idea." He cocked his head. "Did you do anything to agitate it? Maybe stay on it too much?"

Bennie shook her head. "No, I was in bed asleep, and I suddenly woke up in pain."

"It's possible that you turned it the wrong way in your sleep, and then your body registered what was happening." The doctor stepped closer to her. "If you don't mind, I need to examine it."

Bennie grimaced, clutching the sheets. "Okay."

Carefully, he touched her knee in several locations. Bennie grunted, causing Sierra's stomach to tighten. She hated seeing Bennie in so much pain.

Mike stepped back, folding his arms over his chest. "It looks good, better than I expected. There doesn't appear to be much swelling, which is a good sign."

"That's good to hear," Bennie said, sighing in relief. She let out a shaky laugh, the lines around her mouth and eyes deepening. "I just wish it would stop hurting."

A nurse stepped in holding two white pills and a small cup. "Hi, Miss McCain. My name's Lynn. Here, take these for the pain." She rattled off a long technical name of the medication, but it went over Sierra's head.

"We need to take some x-rays just to make sure nothing else is going on," Mike said. "And depending on what those show, we might even do an MRI."

Bennie nodded, a stoic expression on her face. She turned to Sierra and Dalton. "You two must be exhausted." She flashed a contrite grin. "I'm sorry I gave you such a scare."

"No worries," Sierra said quickly. "I'm just glad you're feeling better."

"That's right," Dalton piped in.

A weak smile spread over Bennie's lips. "So am I."

"I have other patients to attend to, but I'll be back in to discuss the results of the x-rays with you," Mike said, leaving the room.

"This will probably take a few hours," Wesley said, touching Bennie's arm. "I can take you home afterwards. That way, Sierra and Dalton won't have to stay."

Sierra's eyes rounded. It was now four a.m. And while she wanted nothing more than to go back and get at least a couple hours of sleep before her meeting, there was no way she was riding back to Sugar Pines with Dalton, alone. "It's okay. I don't mind staying."

"Nonsense," Bennie countered. "You have your meeting later this morning and Dalton has work. You two go on back. Wesley'll take me home."

"Are you sure you'll be okay?" Dalton asked. "I don't mind staying the whole time."

It was touching how concerned Dalton was about Bennie. Sierra had dragged him out of bed in the middle of the night and he'd not uttered a single complaint. Then, it occurred to Sierra that Dalton was probably saying he'd stay because he didn't want to ride home alone with her. For some strange reason, the thought stung.

"I promise, I'll be fine." Bennie reached for Wesley's hand. "I've got this guy to take care of me." She looked up at him and smiled.

"That's right," Wesley said. "You two kids go on home and get some rest. I'll bring Bennie home as soon as everything's done."

Dalton shrugged. "I'd be okay with that." He paused. "But I'm not sure that Sierra feels comfortable riding home alone with me."

She whirled around, shocked Dalton had said that out loud. An open challenge simmered in his eyes as he waited for her to respond.

She detested the heat that crept up her neck. "I don't mind," she heard herself say. She straightened in her seat. "I don't," she said defiantly.

He let out a soft chuckle. "Good, then it's settled."

The note of finality in his voice sent a wave of panic rushing over her. Then she caught the crafty glint in Dalton's eye and knew she'd been played. He knew all he had to do was back her in a corner and she'd come out fighting. That was the trouble with the two of them—they knew each other's weakness and how to push those buttons.

Dalton stood and hugged Bennie. "Get to feeling better, okay?"

She smiled. "Thanks, I will."

Sierra also stood and hugged Bennie. Unexpected tears moistened her eyes. Seeing Bennie in such a terrible state had taken its toll. She couldn't stand the thought of anything happening to Bennie. "Are you sure you'll be okay here?"

"I'll be perfectly fine," Bennie assured her. "See you both at the house."

"Okay."

Dalton looked at her. "You ready?"

"Yep." She forced a smile. *As ready as a lamb going to the slaughter could ever be.*

CHAPTER 10

There were a thousand questions Dalton wanted to ask Sierra, starting with why she'd left him the way she did, but he knew the situation had to be handled with kid gloves. If he pushed too hard, Sierra would clam up. The best way to navigate this was to remain nonchalant.

Sitting in the ER, for one blip of a second, he'd caught a look of longing on Sierra's face as they locked eyes. It made him wonder if she still had feelings for him. The notion had kindled hope in his chest, but he snuffed it out. No way he was going down that road again. She'd hurt him so badly that it nearly destroyed him. It had taken all the grit he could muster to rebuild his life. He couldn't go through that again.

Dalton pushed the key into the ignition and started the engine. Light from the nearby streetlamp flooded into the car. He glanced at Sierra, who had a stony expression. The words came out before he could process what he was saying. "Bennie'll be okay. Wesley's a good guy. He'll take care of her." For the life of him, he couldn't figure out why his first impulse was to jump in and ease Sierra's fears. Pathetic, he knew, but he couldn't seem to help himself.

She cocked her head. "How long have they been together?"

He backed out of the parking space and turned onto the main road. "Wesley and Bennie? I didn't realize they were a couple."

"I thought I saw a spark of something between them."

He shrugged, thinking back to their interaction. The truth was, he'd been so consumed with Sierra that he hardly noticed what was taking place between Bennie and Wesley. "Could be. Wesley's always hanging around."

Silence hung like a dagger between them. Dalton tightened his hold on the steering wheel. At this rate, it was bound to be a long ride home. The essence of Sierra wafted through him, bringing with it a longing so swift it made him dizzy. This woman was doing things to his head. It was hard to be so close to her and not be able to take her in his arms, taste her tantalizing lips. *Okay, enough already!* He turned on the radio and flipped to find a decent station. He left it on classic rock. When a familiar song came on, he started singing along softly. It was nice to have something to divert his attention away from her.

"You sound good," Sierra said when the song ended, "better than before."

He laughed in surprise. "Thanks, I think."

"You always had a wonderful voice, but it's richer now … more defined."

"Or older?"

She chuckled. "That too. Bennie talked about your performances. How long have you been doing that?"

"A couple of years. I started performing in Seattle. My girlfriend at the time was in a band. We used to play and sing together." Now that they were on the road, it was too dark to make out Sierra's expression, but he felt her surprise. He'd wanted to get that out there, so she'd know he was over her.

"What was her name?"

"Miranda."

Long pause. "Why did the two of you break up?"

He let out a humorless laugh, casting a glance at her. "Do you really wanna do this, Sie? Start comparing notes about love interests?"

"I'm just trying to make polite conversation," she snipped. "But if you don't wanna talk, then fine. Have it your way."

He tightened his hold on the steering wheel. "Okay, you wanna play? I'll play. I'll ask a question and you answer it. Then you can ask me one. And we'll go back and forth. Deal?"

"Okay," she said warily. "What do you want to know?"

Why did you leave me? How could you stay away all these years? Did I mean nothing to you? He tightened his jaw, trying to control his emotions. When he spoke, his voice was light. "What is it about your boyfriend that you find so attractive?"

"What? This is ridiculous!" she blustered.

A hard smile curled his lips. "You started it. Now answer the question."

"Well, if you must know, he's ambitious and sophisticated. Parker's a superstar in the advertising world, owns one of the top agencies in the nation."

He grunted. "Prestige was always important to you, wasn't it? More important than people or commitments. The be-all, end-all."

"That's not fair. You make it sound so terrible that I wanted to make something out of myself."

"Actually, I admire that quality about you."

"You do?"

So much for kid gloves. This was going downhill fast. But now that Pandora's Box was opened, there was no reeling his emotions back in. "Yeah, but what I can't tolerate is you pretending to be something you're not."

"What're you talking about?"

"I'm sure you're real proud of yourself, Sie. Got yourself a city boy … your very own Mr. Darcy." He grunted. "Congratulations. It's what you've always wanted."

The music on the radio got drowned out by the strangled sound of Sierra's gasp. "You're a mean, heartless jerk!"

"Yeah, well you're a hoity-toity snob. You know what? I feel sorry for you, Sierra. You keep sitting up there in that glass castle trying to convince yourself that you're happy, when you're actually miserable. It's written all over your face."

"Shut up!" she snarled. "I am happy."

He barked out a laugh. "You keep telling yourself that, darling."

"Pull over!"

He looked at her. "What?"

"I said, *pull over*," she yelled.

"Why?"

"Because I'm not riding in this car another second with you."

His eyes narrowed. "I'm not pulling over. We're on a deserted highway. And you don't even have a cell phone." She shoved him, jerking his hands, causing the car to weave. His stomach lurched as he felt the car slip out of his control. But then he corrected the error. "Are you trying to get us killed?"

"I hate you," she muttered, folding her arms over her chest.

"Yeah, I figured that out the day you deserted me." He couldn't hide the quiver in his voice. It was all out in the open now.

He heard a gurgling sound and realized Sierra was crying. Curse the part of him that wanted to comfort her as he'd done so many times before. What was he supposed to say? *I'm sorry I told the truth?* No words could fix this. Sierra had brought it on herself.

"I'm sorry I hurt you," she finally said.

He swallowed, not believing his ears. His blood pumped faster as he clutched the steering wheel, his eyes fixed on the endless black ribbon of highway before them. "Why did you leave me?" He cringed at the vulnerable tone in his voice, grateful part of his pain remained hidden in the darkness.

"Please, let's not do this." Her voice sounded as haggard and weary as he felt. "I can't," she croaked. "Not now."

Disgust rankled his gut. Of course she'd say that because she didn't want to face it. It was convenient to stay hidden in New York with her perfect boyfriend. Well, he'd make it easier for her. "You know what, it's okay."

She jerked, turning to him. He glanced her direction and even in the near-darkness saw the confusion on her face. "What do you mean?" she asked carefully.

He shrugged, his voice going casual. "I was upset at first. But eventually, I came to realize that you did me a favor."

"I did?" Her voice had a brittle edge to it.

"Yeah." He forced a smile. "I was able to truly start living for myself, rather than feeling obligated to uphold some silly commitment we made as kids."

"I—I see."

He attempted a chuckle, but it came out dry and choked. "I would've told you this years ago. But well … seeing as this is the first time I've seen you … there you go." He was met with a frosty silence that slithered like a python around his heart, but still his tongue wouldn't stop talking. It was like the loose-tongued man on the way to the gallows, bearing his soul to anyone who'd listen. "I've been thinking about why you've been so irate with me."

"I beg your pardon," she said stiffly. "I have not been irate with you." She punched out the words in short bursts.

"Oh, yes, you have. And I think I know why." There was no way he was letting her wiggle out of this one.

She let out a harsh laugh. "Okay, wise guy. Why don't you enlighten me?"

"You're afraid that I'm still carrying a torch for you."

Her voice trembled. "I just want you to be happy … find someone to live your life with, like I have."

The hair on the back of his neck stood. Had she really just said that to him? Find someone like she had? How easily the words slipped through her lips. She might as well have been talking about switching to a new pair of shoes. "You don't have to worry about that, darling. It's already done."

"What?"

He smiled a little at the shock in her voice. It felt good to give it back to her. "Yes, darling, I'm dating someone. So you have nothing to worry about." Sierra would blow her cork when she realized who that girl was.

"Oh ... good." Long Pause. "Who are you dating?"

"Now, honey, you know I don't kiss and tell," he drawled.

He turned into the driveway of Bennie's mansion and drove around to the back. Then he turned off the car. "I'm glad we had this little talk."

"Yeah, me too." She forced a smile. "Thanks for the ride back. And thanks again for helping Bennie." Her voice had a false cheerfulness like she was talking to a stranger.

He nodded. "Anytime."

They both got out of the car.

A crooked grin slid over his lips. "Now that wasn't so bad, was it? It feels good to clear the air."

"Yes," she agreed, but didn't look happy about it. She looked down-right ticked. For someone who didn't care a hoot about him, she certainly wasn't acting like it. He got a perverse sense of satisfaction out of knowing she was jealous. It was nice to turn the tables for once.

"Here, catch." He tossed her the keys. As they stood looking at each other, Dalton felt his heart whither—a lifetime of hopes and dreams crumbling to the ground like dust. How could it still hurt this bad ... even after all these years? She was so beautiful—strong, yet fragile. How well he knew her face, the stubborn tilt of her chin, the purity in her liquid blue eyes.

Everything in him wanted to grab her and shake some sense into her, then kiss her senseless. He wanted to hold her close and never let her go. Before he'd fallen in love with Sierra, she was his best friend. He caught the wistful look in her eyes, could tell she was fighting a doozy of an inner battle. Why wouldn't she let him in, so he could help her? The answer came lightning fast—because he was the battle, that's why.

Somehow, he knew that if he went to her this moment, she wouldn't be able to resist him. But where would that leave him? Because while she wouldn't leave him today, she would eventually leave, just as she'd done before. Habit took over as Dalton did the one thing he knew would put space between them—the thing he needed to protect himself from doing something stupid. A cocky grin slid like molasses over his lips. "Do you need me to help you inside? Make sure the boogey man's not hiding under the bed?" That was an inside joke between the two of them when they were growing up. Dalton used the boogey man as an excuse to come over and "keep her safe."

Her head shot up, eyes blazing. "That won't be necessary."

"Yeah, it looks like you've done a pretty good job of fighting off the boogey man on your own." He saluted. "See ya around, Sie."

Before she could answer, he turned on his heel and strode away.

CHAPTER 11

Sierra's head felt like it had been bludgeoned with a bat. After this call was over, she was going back to the mansion to get a few hours of sleep so she'd feel human again. Thankfully, Bennie was doing well. The MRI showed that the ligament was healing nicely; leading the doctor to believe Bennie had simply slept wrong on her knee. This was a huge relief. Bennie asked her to call Dalton and let him know, but Sierra told Bennie she could call him herself. The less contact Sierra had with Dalton, the better.

Who was he dating? Did she know the girl? It stung to think that Dalton didn't care that Sierra had left him. To think, all these years she'd harbored such agonizing guilt for how everything had gone down, and he didn't even give a crap. She couldn't help chuckling at the irony.

"I take it, from the ideas you sent over, you think Pristine Pizza should take a more modern, streamlined approach," Parker said.

"Uh, yeah." She jerked back to attention, focusing on the screen. Parker and the five members of her team were sitting around the conference room table, staring at the screen on the wall that patched into her. For a few minutes, the conversation had centered on demographics from key areas around the nation where Pristine Pizza was hoping to capture a larger market share. Originating in Portland, Oregon, the restaurant chain had a grunge feel, catering to Millennials. Ross, the owner, wanted his restaurants to "grow up" and reach a larger market. To do this, the brand and restaurant designs needed a complete overhaul.

"Would you mind explaining your thought process to the team?" Parker asked.

Her pulse picked up a notch. *Thought process?* She wet her lips, attempting to collect her thoughts enough to convey something halfway intelligent. *No golden nuggets yet ...* unfortunately. She tried to sound more confident than she felt. "Going with a modern look would make the restaurants feel more upscale. And maybe they could incorporate a few healthy pizzas and salads as well."

"Did you have a color scheme in mind?" This came from Angie, the head graphic artist.

"No, not really. I'd like to do some more research." A trickle of sweat rolled between Sierra's shoulders. "Do any of you have ideas?" She was shooting in the dark here, totally unprepared.

"Normally, when you think of modern and streamlined, you think of whites," Bill said.

Parker frowned. "That seems cold and sterile for a pizza place." He looked at Sierra, his brow creasing in concern. "Are you sure modern is the right approach? What does your market research indicate? Do you have any comparisons you could show us?"

Her breath hitched. "Um, I haven't had a chance to really delve into that yet." Her voice trailed off when she saw the look of disappointment on Parker's face. For a split second, she feared he might chew her out, right here in front of the team, but he blew out a long breath, tugging at his ear. She knew that unconscious gesture. Parker was getting nervous.

"Okay," Parker said. "Let's put that aspect on hold for a few minutes and jump to the campaign. What are your thoughts for that?"

All eyes turned to Sierra, awaiting her answer. *Sheesh.* Was she the only one with an opinion? Normally, she would've spent a full day researching the topic and would have had a plan down to the letter. But seeing as how she'd been out all last night ... and that her mind was a jumble over Dalton ... she was at a complete loss. Her eye caught on the little boy sitting at a nearby table with his mother. When he realized Sierra was looking at him, he stuck out his tongue and stuffed his thumbs in his ears, wiggling his fingers like antlers. His mother swatted his head before mouthing an apology.

Sierra chuckled. "No worries." She glanced around the room and noticed a few people watching her. Even though she'd chosen a table in the corner, she was still causing quite the spectacle with her computer open, doing a Skype call.

"I'm sorry?" Parker said.

"Oh, nothing." She looked at the boy again. This time, he grinned sheepishly and waved. She shook her head, smiling back. The boy leaned over and noisily slurped his strawberry shake. She glanced at the pre-teen girls sitting on the red-lacquer barstools, their legs swinging back and forth as they ate their mile-high sundaes.

Clydedale's was the embodiment of everything Sierra loved about small town living. The fragrant smell of dough mingling with spicy marinara tingled her senses, causing her stomach to rumble. She'd ordered a soda when she first got here but hadn't had time to get anything to eat. After the Skype call was over, she planned to order her favorite—a pepperoni, hand-tossed pizza with extra cheese. Her gaze took in the black and white checked floor, fire-engine red barstools beside the counter, the old-fashion candy jars on the wooden shelves, large metal road signs on the walls, the large windows in front with the morning sun streaming in.

Parker cleared his throat. "Are you with us?"

"Yeah, I'm here." She realized with a start they were waiting for her to answer. What was the question? Oh, yeah, the marketing venue. "Maybe a combination of radio and Internet?"

"As opposed to TV?" Parker asked.

"TV is certainly effective, but pricey," she countered. "And Ross iterated that he wanted his advertising budget to stretch as far as possible. We could start with radio and Internet, then follow that up with a print campaign."

"Sounds reasonable," Parker said. Mary, his assistant, nodded and jotted it down.

Sierra's shoulders relaxed. At least she'd said something right.

Parker leaned back in his seat. "Now back to the design. Once we nail that down, we can come up with a slogan."

"The taste of home in every bite," Sierra blurted.

Parker cocked his head. "What?"

"That's the slogan." A laugh gurgled in her throat. The answer had been right in front of her the entire time, but she was too stupid to see it. "I don't think we should do modern."

Parker's brows scrunched. "But you just said—"

She waved a hand. "I know what I said," she said impatiently, "but that's not the right approach. Everyone's going modern. We need to go the other direction." She glanced around. "We need an old-fashioned, pizza/soda shop feel. A place where families can come together and hang out." She began describing the restaurant around her. "A place that feels like home." When the words ran dry, she sat back and waited for their reactions.

A broad smile split Parker's face. "The taste of home in every bite," he repeated. "I love it. It's ingenious. You had me worried for a minute there, but it's brilliant."

All Sierra could feel right now was a heady relief. Her head was pounding. She needed sleep! The door opened. Her jaw dropped when Dalton strolled in. He looked at her, giving her a slight smile of acknowledgement. *Crap!* She didn't want Parker to see Dalton. He'd take one look at the two of them and know something was up. No, that was ridiculous. Nothing was going on! Dalton didn't care a hoot about her. He was dating someone else.

It was then that she saw a flash of blonde hair and realized Dalton was with a woman, presumably the one he was dating. She stepped up beside him and linked her arm through his. Then she leaned close and laughed at something he'd said. Sierra's eyes took it all in like a snapshot before her brain could connect the dots. Glossy hair, beautiful features, stylish outfit, petite and shapely.

Three words formed in her mind, sending a sliver of horror running down her spine. Ivie Jane Compton! Her best friend turned nemesis. The one who could never forgive Sierra for what her mother had done. Sierra's stomach rolled onto the floor in a putrid glob as a dart of jealousy stabbed through her heart with such intensity that it nearly took her breath away.

"Are you okay?" Parker asked. "What's going on there?"

A rubbery smile twisted over her lips. "I'm fine. Hey, sorry, but I'm gonna have to let you go." Shakes started in her hands, moving up her body.

"But we still have a good two-hour's worth of work in front of us. We need to nail down the logo and color scheme," he argued. "Get some basic copy down. We have to be ready to present something to Ross tomorrow when he comes in."

"Black, white, and red," Sierra rattled off. "I've already given you the slogan. Bill, you should be able to come up with some copy. Just keep it family oriented—a place where families want to be. Think of the old-fashioned soda shops with the gleaming counters and chrome accents."

He nodded. "Got it."

"Angie, I'll give you leeway to work your magic on the logo. Shoot me a few samples by the end of the day."

"Will do."

Crap! They were coming towards her. "Sorry, but I've got to sign off now." She flashed a brief smile at Parker. "I'll catch up with you later today." She ended the call just as Dalton and Ivie Jane approached the table.

"Good morning," Dalton said cheerfully, a slow smile sliding over his lips. Unlike her, he didn't look like he'd been up most of the night. He was fresh … and gorgeous in a mid-tone grey button-down shirt that caught the color of his eyes. Not to mention the fact that it showcased his sculpted body. She allowed herself one tiny glance at his cut biceps. *Sheesh.* Did he live in a gym?

Dalton looked her up and down, and she could sense his disapproval. She was wearing jeans and a plain t-shirt. Her hair was skinned back in a ponytail, and she barely had on any makeup. Ivie Jane, on the other hand, looked like she'd just stepped out of a magazine. She had to fight the urge to scowl.

Amusement lit Dalton's eyes as he motioned. "I see you've set up shop."

"Yeah, I needed the Internet," she responded dryly.

He chuckled, the sound vibrating in Sierra's chest. "Oh, that's right. Bennie has a vendetta against the Internet, refuses to spend money on it. You're always welcome to go to my office across the street. I'm sure Phyllis would love the company."

She caught the glint in his eyes, knew he was needling her. "As wonderful as that sounds, I think I'll stay here," she said sweetly.

He shrugged. "Suit yourself."

Sierra hated the way her cells came alive now that Dalton was in the room. She caught a trace of his clean, masculine scent with a hint of musk. Or maybe it was her imagination. Maybe her mind was filling in the gaps from before. But whatever was happening, it was dang frustrating.

Sierra looked at Ivie Jane who was studying her intently, like she was a bug under a microscope. Let's see, the last time they'd spoken was in the cafeteria during their junior year in high school. Ivie Jane called Sierra a scumbag who wouldn't amount to a hill of beans. That was right before Sierra punched her. She'd gotten suspended for three days, but it was so worth it.

"Hey, Sierra," Ivie Jane said, a breezy note in her voice. "It's been a long time."

"Yes, it has." Not long enough in Sierra's opinion. Sierra was terribly sorry that her mother took the life of Ivie Jane's mother but there wasn't a dang thing she could do about it.

Ivie Jane gave Dalton an adoring look. "This guy told me you were back in town," she cooed.

Sierra's stomach roiled at the sight of the two of them together. Was this some sort of twisted joke? Or nightmare? Of all the people for him to date, why did it have to be her greatest rival? "Yeah, I came back to help my aunt," she said stiffly.

"Nadine's been in contact with me about the catering. I think it'll work out well for all of us." Ivie Jane smiled, but her eyes remained cold. Sierra knew in that moment that Ivie Jane hated her as much now as she ever did. She'd just learned the art of masking her hatred in good, old-fashioned southern hospitality—hand you the casserole with one hand and twist the knife in your back with the other.

Ivie Jane motioned to Sierra's ponytail. "That's an interesting look. A kind of urban, city thing," she twanged.

Sierra smiled humorlessly. "Thanks. Ponytails are the rage in New York," she said dryly.

Dalton's eyes widened a fraction and the corners of his lips quivered like he was trying not to laugh. For some strange reason, an incredulous laugh rose in her throat as her eyes met his. She felt that same age-old connection buzz between them like an electrical current. Ivie Jane noticed it too and cut her eyes at Dalton.

"Well," she sniffed. "It's nice seeing you, Sierra." She spoke her name like it was a swear word. "Good luck back in New York," she chimed.

Sierra could tell Ivie Jane would've ridden her out of town on a rail that instant if she could've.

"Good to see you too," Sierra repeated, mimicking Ivie Jane's buttery tone. Then she flashed a smile so big it made her cheeks hurt.

Ivie Jane tugged on Dalton's arm. "Let's get something to eat. I'm starved."

"I'm surprised you're eating here instead of your own restaurant," Sierra said.

"My restaurant only opens for dinner," Ivie Jane countered snippily like Sierra had made a dumb remark.

"Let's go, hon," Ivie Jane said.

Dalton nodded, but his feet stayed rooted on the floor. Ivie cocked her head in a question. "There was something else I wanted to tell you," he mused. He looked at Ivie, then back to Sierra. "Oh, yeah. I know what it was. Janie wanted to invite you to her dad's birthday party a week from Saturday at six p.m."

The stunned look on Ivie Jane's face was comical, sending a smile over Sierra's lips. Then she realized Dalton had called her Janie, a nickname suggesting an added layer of affection between them. She scowled inwardly.

"It would be a nice gesture of goodwill," Dalton added.

Sierra's eyes narrowed. What was she? Some charity case?

Ivie managed to pick the corners of her smile back up. "Of course, we'd love to have you at the party."

"Thanks, but I think I have other plans." There was no way Sierra was going to that party.

Dalton frowned. "That's too bad. It would be a great opportunity to promote the play. I'm sure Janie wouldn't mind letting you announce it. Right, babe?"

Seriously? First Janie and then babe? Sierra wanted to puke. "I'll think about it," she said, mostly because she could see how flustered Ivie Jane was. She still couldn't believe Dalton was dating her. The ultimate betrayal!

His eyes locked with hers, sending a smolder into her stomach. "See ya around."

She nodded. "Bye." She watched them walk to a table and sit down. Her emotions were a tangled mass of ropes with no ends. She didn't care whom Dalton dated. Of course she was surprised that he was dating Ivie Jane. But more power to them. She tried to avoid looking at them as she forced her eyes to her screen. She didn't know how many minutes passed before someone spoke.

"This is for you." She looked up in surprise as Clyde Roberts, the owner of the restaurant placed a piping-hot pepperoni and cheese pizza on the table.

"But I didn't order anything," she protested, her stomach rumbling. Crazy that she lived in New York where a person could theoretically get some of the best pizza in the US, but as far as Sierra was concerned, nothing compared to this.

"On the house," he winked.

"Thank you." She felt a rush of tenderness for the balding man in his mid-sixties who'd always been super kind. He and his wife Dale ran the restaurant, hence the name Clydedale's. He had on the same attire he'd worn for as long as she'd known him—a white round-neck t-shirt and jeans. A cream apron, stained with pizza sauce, was stretched over his round belly. Sierra closed her laptop and pushed it off to the side. "You brought my favorite." She was impressed that he still remembered after all these years.

"Of course." He perched a hand on his hip. "You and Dalton were two of my best customers." He chuckled. "I remember the time y'all put away three whole pizzas."

That was the day Sierra made a proper English brunch, complete with cucumber sandwiches and tea. She insisted that Dalton join her. Dalton took one bite and gagged, but Sierra argued they were good and that Dalton wasn't cultured enough to appreciate them. After the first square, however, she couldn't do it any longer. They tasted like wet sponges. Finally, Dalton grabbed those sandwiches and flung them across the yard. Sierra was mad at first, then broke out laughing. Afterwards, they were still starving so they came here and scarfed down the pizzas. "That was a lifetime ago," she said glumly, stealing a glance at Dalton and Ivie Jane. Nothing was the same as it had been before. An inexplicable feeling of loss overtook her, sending moisture into her eyes. Rapidly, she blinked it away.

Clyde touched her arm. "He still loves you," he said softly.

She jerked. "Huh?"

"A few minutes ago, I watched him talking to you. It's written all over his face ..." he gave her a pointed look "...and yours." His expression grew reflective. "I've seen a lot of people come and go over the years, but I've never seen a couple as much in love as the two of you. Dale and I were just talking about it the other day. You're soulmates. Always have been ... always will be."

Sierra couldn't stop the tear from rolling down her cheek. She swiped it away. "Thanks for the pizza," she said hoarsely. "Please tell Dale I said *hello*." *Hold it together*, she commanded herself. *Don't give Dalton and Ivie Jane the pleasure of seeing you fall apart.*

He looked her in the eye. "If a love's worth having, it's worth fighting for." He made a clicking sound with this tongue as he slapped the table and winked. "Remember what I said, okay?"

She nodded, her eyes burning. Mechanically, she reached for a slice of pizza and took a bite, not tasting a thing.

CHAPTER 12

"*F*antastic. Thank you. I look forward to seeing you tomorrow."

Sierra pumped her fist and let out a little shout of exultation as she ended the call. She glanced at Bennie whose nose was buried in the script for *Macbeth*. "That makes three appointments set up with tourist companies tomorrow."

"That's nice," Bennie said absently, pushing her glasses higher up on her nose.

"One would think you'd be a little happier, since I'm saving your bacon," Sierra muttered.

"The mansion, dear. You're saving it, not my bacon," Bennie retorted.

Sierra rolled her eyes. "Same thing." She was making progress. Next, she needed to head outside and snap a few pictures of the outdoor theater. Then she'd write some copy and compile everything into a PowerPoint presentation. "Do you have bios of all the actors in the play?"

Bennie looked over her glasses. "Yes, I do. Would you like for me to make you a copy?"

She was thinking it would be nice to have it in electronic form so she wouldn't have to retype it, but that was a stretch for Bennie. "A copy would be nice," she finally said.

After she'd come back from Clydedale's she lay down and slept for a couple of hours, then felt much better. Parker called her right after she woke up. He complimented her design idea for Pristine Pizza, then he asked if she was doing okay.

"I'm fine. Why?"

"I dunno. You just seem a little distant. Is your aunt okay?"

"Yeah, she's a tough old bird." She didn't go into the details of all that had happened the night before with the hospital and Dalton.

"How much longer do you think you'll be there?"

"I'm not sure," she hedged. She'd have to find a way to tell Parker the truth. But four weeks … that seemed so freaking long, even to her. How was she supposed to explain it to Parker? She hated the strain coming between them, even after two days. What would it be like several weeks from now? She'd believed that she and Parker had a strong relationship, but now? Now, she wasn't sure of anything. How could everything fall apart in two measly days?

She was still smarting from seeing Dalton with Ivie Jane. And then there were Clyde's strange comments. He meant well, but he couldn't know how much he'd shaken her. Was she still in love with Dalton? She trembled at the thought, partly out of fear and partly out of desire. No, it was just fear!

The doorbell rang once before the door burst open. "Hello," Nadine boomed, stepping into the office. "It's just me. I made you some turtles." She smiled at Sierra. "I know how much you love them."

She took the white box from Nadine. "Thank you. That was so nice of you." She did love Nadine's turtles. It was an interesting feeling to be surrounded by people who knew her so well, even though she'd been away from them for years. She thought she'd changed so much, but maybe at the core she was still the same uncertain girl she'd always been. Had she built Parker up to be more than he was? Over-looked his flaws so she could make him into the perfect guy she'd been seeking since youth? She wasn't sure of anything anymore.

Nadine waved a hand. "Oh, it wasn't any trouble."

She sat down in a chair and primly crossed her legs, adjusting her pants so the crease was straight. Her black eyes flickered over Sierra and Bennie. "What're you girls up to?"

"Sierra's working on promotion for the play, and I'm going over blocking for the script. Landon asked for my help. I've got a few music students coming this afternoon, starting at three." She paused. "I'm surprised to see you here."

"I took the day off."

"That's nice." Bennie placed the script on the desk, turning her full attention to Nadine.

Nadine looked a little older than Sierra remembered, but not much. Her short black hair had a few more streaks of gray and the lines around her eyes were more pronounced. But that was about it. Nadine was a sharp dresser and well educated. She spoke French. And when she wasn't working at the bank, traveled overseas with her husband, Hal. Now that Sierra had been exposed to the glamour of the city, Nadine didn't seem larger than life like she did when Sierra was a kid. But still, she was a very classy lady.

"What're you doing on your day off? Besides making candy and visiting us?" Bennie asked.

Nadine's eyes sparkled. "Hal and I are heading into Charleston to see the symphony."

Sierra had a hard time picturing Hal at the symphony. He was a country boy through and through, much more comfortable watching a football game on TV while popping open a cold beer. But he dearly loved Nadine and was happy to take her wherever she wanted to go.

Nadine gave Sierra a speculative look.

"What?" Sierra tugged at her shirt, wishing she'd taken the time to fix herself up a little more today.

"So, I spoke to Phyllis Watson."

Crap! Not good. She braced herself for what was sure to come.

"She said you and Dalton had a fender bender yesterday."

Bennie peered over her glasses. "What? Is that the accident you and Dalton were talking about last night?"

"Yes," Sierra admitted, feeling like she was ten years old again and had just gotten in trouble for tracking mud over the carpet. "I ran into the back of Dalton's truck."

Bennie gave her a censuring look. "Why didn't you tell me?"

"Your friends were here, and I didn't want to worry you …" she pointed to Bennie's knee "… under the circumstances."

Bennie clucked her tongue, shaking her head. "I'm glad you are both okay."

"Yeah, me too." They were paranoid about car accidents after what happened to Sierra's mother.

Nadine gave Sierra a pointed look. "How are things with Dalton?"

Sierra tensed. "What do you mean?"

"Well, Bennie said he came over for dinner last night." Nadine tucked a strand of hair behind her ear, revealing gold, coin-shaped earrings.

"To discuss the set design," Sierra countered. Nadine's hawk-eyes scoped her for any sign of weakness. *Be strong*, she commanded herself.

"And then you rode home from the hospital together," Nadine continued.

Sierra saw the spark of interest in Bennie's eyes. "What is this? The Spanish Inquisition?" she mumbled, her face going hot. She felt like the two of them could see right through her and knew she still had feelings for Dalton.

"Don't get your panties in a wad," Bennie laughed. "Nadine's just asking a simple question. How did it go?" she repeated.

Sierra rolled her eyes. "All right, I guess." *Geez*. "We were thrown together due to circumstance. We got along okay, I guess … considering that we're both dating other people." She smiled inwardly when Bennie's face fell. Yep, she was still playing matchmaker, refusing to give up on the idea of Sierra and Dalton getting back together. "By the way, I didn't realize Dalton and Ivie Jane were dating." The words cut leaving her mouth.

Nadine waved a hand, her expression going sour. "Yeah, I don't see that lasting. Ivie Jane's a talented woman, and her restaurant's outstanding. But Dalton's way out of her league."

Sierra jerked like she'd been slapped. Then she pinned Nadine with a look. "What did you say?"

Nadine squirmed in her seat. "Only that I don't think Dalton and Ivie Jane are well suited for each other."

She leaned forward. "Don't you mean that Dalton isn't good enough for Ivie Jane? Or me? That's what you said shortly before I left for New York, remember?" Nadine told her that if she remained in this town with Dalton that she'd end up just like her mother, a drunk. When Sierra said that Dalton could change—had promised profusely that he would change, Nadine argued that a zebra couldn't change his stripes. "He'll promise you the world and leave you in ruin," Nadine finished. Those words had seared into Sierra's soul, were the impetus for her transformation.

"Um …" Nadine's face drained as she moistened her lips. "About that." She laughed hesitantly. "Those things I said … I may have been wrong."

Sierra's head burned like it was splitting in two. "'May have been wrong?'" She gritted her teeth. "What're you saying?"

"Dalton's not the man I assumed he was." She clenched her hands. "He's a much better man than I realized." Her voice trailed off.

Sierra clutched her neck, an incredulous laugh building in her throat. "How can you sit there and say that to me?" The room started to spin. What the heck was happening to her? She couldn't believe Nadine would have the audacity to sing such a different tune. "No!" She shook her head. "I took your advice and left Dalton. I built a new life." The walls closed in on her. "I'm happy with my life in New York. I love Parker." An icy fear trickled down her spine as she clutched the arms of the chair. Even in her own ears, the words came out sounding like a lie. She detested the looks of pity on Nadine and Bennie's faces. "What about the alcohol?" she half shouted.

Nadine looked at Bennie who nodded for her to continue. "He no longer drinks. Hasn't touched a drop for several years now."

Tears stung Sierra's eyes. "Really?" she squeaked. She shook her head. "Even if I wanted to get back together with Dalton …" she held up a hand "…and I'm not saying that I do. But at any rate, it's too late.

Dalton and I live in different worlds. He's with someone else." The words fell like daggers from her lips as she scowled. "Ivie Jane Compton. Of all people," she muttered. "The one person who made my life a living nightmare."

"Ivie Jane's mixed up," Bennie said. "She had no right to treat you the way she did. She was hurt and took it out on you. The whole thing's just so unfortunate. If Claire only knew all the trouble she caused."

Sierra's mind was spinning out of control. Dalton no longer drank? He'd built a good life for himself—was a good person. She didn't know what to do with this. She couldn't deny that she still had feelings for Dalton. And now she knew she'd made a terrible mistake by leaving him. She should've never listened to Nadine. Regret pumped poison through her veins, squeezing her heart to the size of a marble. What was done was done. Even if she wanted to start over with Dalton, she couldn't. Dalton was glad Sierra had left him. He told her that point blank. He was with Ivie Jane now. And her life was in New York with Parker. Not here.

Suddenly, she had to leave. She stood. "Excuse me," she mumbled, fleeing the room.

CHAPTER 13

*D*alton leaned against the rungs of the ladder and used his body weight to press the nail gun against the wood as he pumped a line of nails along the bottom of the crown molding. The idea was to keep the set design as simple as possible and yet still be effective for the play. Also, the materials had to be able to withstand the elements.

After lunch at Clydedale's, Dalton dropped Janie off at her restaurant, then went to a couple of sites to check on the progress of his jobs. Next, he came here to the outdoor theater to get started on the set. He'd hoped that Hank Trenton would've gotten more accomplished before he had to pull away from the project to look after his wife, Mandy.

Truthfully, it would've been easier to just start from scratch rather than trying to correct the sections Hank built. Everything was so out of whack and crooked that it was doubtful Hank had used a level. Had this been for anyone but Bennie, Dalton would've been tempted to bow out of the job. But there was no way he could leave Bennie in the lurch. He'd just have to do his best to piece the thing together and hope it would last through the performances.

He stepped down the ladder and put down the nail gun, wiping his hand across his brow. Thank goodness, the weather hadn't been terribly hot the past few weeks, just upper eighties during the heat of the day. This evening, it was cooler than normal. A restless energy moved through the air signaling an approaching storm. He'd have to hurry and get as much done as he could before the rain set in.

Even though the rain would hinder his progress, he loved the powerful weather fronts that moved in and out of the low-country like stomping giants. He cast an appreciative glance around the perimeter of the outdoor theater, his eye moving up the height of the majestic live oaks that watched over the land like silent guardians. This really was a beautiful spot. He'd taken it for granted as a kid, but now he knew what a blessing it was that he was able to purchase the Drexel mansion.

He leaned over and picked up several of the sections of wood he'd cut earlier. They'd make up the treads on the two staircases leading to the raised section with the pillars and three-piece crown molding. Hank had cut the stringer or framework for the stairs. Dalton would have to place the treads over it, then check each one to make sure each was level before nailing it into place. It would be a tedious process as he'd have to carve out sections of the stringer to level the treads. But with any luck, he'd have at least one staircase done before the rain hit.

It was nice being out here working with his hands because it gave him time to think. His business had evolved to the point where Dalton mostly managed projects rather than doing any of the manual labor. And while he enjoyed interacting with clients, he sometimes missed the simplicity of a hard day of physical work.

His thoughts wandered over the events of the day. It was strange being with Janie at Clydedale's with Sierra in the same room watching. Yeah, he'd noticed that Sierra's eyes were glued to him and Janie, even though she tried hard to act disinterested. Dalton kept replaying the shocked look on Sierra's face when she saw him with Janie. He'd assumed it would give him a sense of vindication to flaunt Janie in front of Sierra, but it just felt awkward. And wrong. He'd been so preoccupied with Sierra that he felt like he was in a dense fog.

Janie noticed that something was wrong and asked if he was okay.

He blamed his aloofness on lack of sleep from the events of the night before. The excuse somewhat mollified Janie, but it wouldn't for long. Janie was understandably nervous about Sierra coming back to Sugar Pines. And while it wasn't Janie's style to come right out and ask Dalton if he still had feelings for Sierra, he could tell she wondered.

Technically, Dalton and Janie weren't exclusive, although neither of them had been dating other people. Dalton was relieved Janie hadn't confronted him with the question because he didn't want to tell her a lie, and he couldn't admit the truth. He'd never stopped loving Sierra. He knew that now more than ever. And maybe it was wishful thinking, but he was starting to suspect that Sierra felt the same way.

He'd not planned to invite Sierra to Janie's dad's birthday party. The words had slipped out. But once he extended the invitation, he realized that he wanted Sierra there. If only just to be in the same area with her. He considered making up an excuse to visit Bennie this evening, just so he could see Sierra.

The wind picked up and roused the monstrous tree branches into action, swaying the Spanish Moss back and forth like synchronized pendulums. And with the wind came the faint scent of magnolia blooms. He loved being outside. He missed the beach. Even though it was only fifteen miles away, it was hard to break away from work to get there. He needed to go soon. Janie had been bugging him to take her, but he'd put it off. The beach had been his and Sierra's playground, their haven. He wasn't ready to share that with anyone else. Better to go alone. He probably wouldn't go to the lighthouse because that would be too painful to do without Sierra at his side. But he could at least walk on the beach, take a swim in the ocean.

He was on his knees, bent over the staircase after placing the first board on the stringer, and was holding the level next to it when he heard a rustle. He turned, surprised to see the object of his thoughts standing before him.

"Sierra?"

It flashed through his mind that she'd changed clothes and fixed her hair and makeup. Man, she looked good. Her voluminous hair fell in soft rings over her slender shoulders. His gaze took in her silky skin, her heart-shaped lips painted cinnamon red to match her hair. For a second, all thoughts flew from his mind as he got lost in the mystery of her large blue eyes. Then he realized that he must look like a goober gawking at her. He rose to his feet, his blood pumping faster. "Hey," he drawled, his trademark grin slipping over his lips like an old friend to hide his jitters. He felt like he was sixteen again, reliving his first crush. He chuckled inwardly at the bad analogy. Sierra had been his first crush … his only crush.

"Hey." Her eyes swept over the set. "It looks great."

"So do you," he murmured. It was fun to watch color creep into her cheeks. He probably shouldn't have said that, but he couldn't seem to resist. At least he had the power to illicit some sort of reaction from her.

She lowered her eyes, her lashes brushing against her cheek-bones. It was amazing how seductive that simple action was. The thin fabric of her white blouse traced the outline of her slim figure. The collar was open, revealing her delicate neck and collarbone. Her jeans were faded and ripped in the knees. The bottoms were rolled up, showing her ankles and denim wedge sandals dotted with rhinestones.

This morning, she'd been cute in a granola way with her hair in a ponytail. But tonight, she was a walking felony. Was she going out? Her boyfriend was still in New York, wasn't he? A surge of jealousy spiked through him sending a poisonous anger coursing through his veins. No other man had the right to claim Sierra as his own. She'd belonged with him since they were kids. Or at least he thought that was the case until she left. *It takes two to tango,* his mind yelled. No matter how much he loved or wanted Sierra, if she didn't feel the same way, it was a dead-end street.

"I thought I'd better come out and get an idea of what we're dealing with." She spoke fast, like she needed to explain why she was here. He watched as she picked at her fingernails. In the old days, she chewed on her nails when she was nervous.

He chuckled. "You can come out here anytime you want. And you certainly don't have to give me an explanation." The words came out casually, like he couldn't care less what she did.

She jutted out her chin, her eyes sparking. "I wasn't. I was just making conversation."

"Okay," he said nonchalantly. He strode over and picked up his nail gun, then shot the nails into the wood. It sounded like bullets whizzing by. He could feel her eyes, watching him. He placed another section of wood on the stringer and checked it with the level. This one was off by a half inch. He sighed. He'd have to chisel away a section of wood on the right side. It was hard to concentrate with her so close.

"Do you need any help?"

He couldn't stop the laugh from escaping his throat. "I beg your pardon."

She motioned. "With the steps." Her eyes met his, and he caught the hint of defiance in them that seemed to be saying, *You won't dismiss me with that good ol' boy indifference.*

He looked her up and down, allowing himself a quick pause on the curve of her hips and long legs before flickering back to her face. An amused grin tugged at his lips. "Dressed like that?"

She put a hand on her hip, challenge simmering in her eyes. "Do you want my help or not?"

His blood zinged excitement through his veins. What was it about this woman that made him feel so totally and completely alive? He cocked an eyebrow. "All right, Sie," he murmured. "Let's see what ya got." He pointed to his toolbox. "There's a chisel in the top tray. Would you get it for me?"

"Sure."

Out of the corner of his eye, he watched her walk. Her movements were fluid, graceful, her hair bouncing on her shoulders as she went. A couple of seconds later, she returned, handing it to him.

"Thanks," he said offhandedly.

"What're you using it for?"

She seemed genuinely interested in what he was doing. "For this." He began chipping away the wood. "The stringer's off. I'm trying to make it level so the stairs won't be crooked."

She laughed. "Yeah, that wouldn't be good. I can see the actors now." She stretched her neck, her voice going lofty as she straightened to her full height and held out her arms in a grand motion as she began quoting, "'Out, out, brief candle! Life's but a walking shadow, a poor player that struts and frets his hour upon the stage and then is heard no more.'" She giggled, placing her hand over her mouth. "Because he fell and busted his head during the first scene of the second act."

He couldn't help but snigger. "Impressive," he grunted. "Which play was that from?"

"*Macbeth*, of course. Bennie's favorite. Well, second to *The Merchant of Venice*, that is. But audiences usually prefer Macbeth's paranoia to Shylock's demand for a pound of Antonio's flesh."

He arched an eyebrow. "Since when did you become an expert on Shakespeare? The girl I knew hated Bennie's plays."

"Still do," she muttered. "But you can't live with Bennie and not soak a little of it in." She sighed like she was having some inner dialogue with herself. Then she motioned. "Don't let me keep you from working." She looked up at the darkening clouds. "You don't have much time before the bottom falls out."

He pursed his lips. "About forty-five minutes, I'm guessing."

Her eyes widened, then a playful smile tugged at her lips. "Nah, thirty minutes. Tops."

He felt himself grin, a genuine one this time. "What's the wager?" When they were kids, they used to lie on the grass and watch the thunderclouds roll in, taking bets on when the first drops of rain would fall. "A kiss?" he said softly, searching her face. That had most often been the prize Dalton wanted. Her jaw dropped as she clenched her hands, making him think he'd pushed too far. But then she laughed.

"I guess I set myself up for that one, huh?"

He nodded. "Pretty much."

She tilted her head, looking thoughtful. "How about a walk instead?"

"A walk?" he asked dubiously.

"If I win, we take a walk together. Down by old man Shutter's place. I've been wanting to go back there, but I'm afraid to go by myself ... with the snakes." She made a face. "And who knows what other creatures rustling around in the grass."

"To the swimming hole?" He broke into a large smile. "You up for a little skinny dipping, Sie?"

Her face turned beet red as she held up a finger. "No, just a walk. My skinny-dipping days are definitely over." She straightened her shoulders, a prim look molding over her features. "I'm a changed woman now."

"Too bad," he murmured. "Okay, a walk it is, if you win. Which I highly doubt." He grinned. "I'll be sure and carry a big stick to ward off the snakes." He gave her a meaningful look. "And any boogey men we might encounter."

She grunted, but he caught the smile in her eyes. He didn't know what had changed in the past few hours, but it was like the old Sierra was returning ... his Sierra. He tipped his head, his tone going musing. "Let's see ..." He put a finger to his lips. "What do I want? Other than a kiss, of course?" Her eyes connected with his sending a jolt of adrenaline through him. "If I win, we go into Charleston for a nice dinner." And maybe a walk on the beach afterwards, he added to himself.

She rocked back. "I—I don't think that's a good idea."

He shrugged. "A kiss or dinner. Your choice."

She laughed, giving him an admiring look. "All right, wise guy. You're on. For dinner ... that is." She pulled her phone from her back pocket. "Time starts now."

"I see how you are."

"What?"

"We've spent a good three to five minutes talking about it. You have to deduct that from the time."

"Fine," she sniffed, rolling her eyes. "You're so picky."

"Just keeping you honest." How easy it was for them to fall back into their old banter.

She made a flourish with her hand. "Chop, chop. Slow poke." She looked at the clouds, her eyes dancing wickedly. "I feel the rain coming on," she drawled. "You're sooo gonna lose this one."

He returned to his task, even though his mind was no longer on it, but on the captivating redhead standing beside him. Sierra had always been a beautiful woman, but she'd really come into her own. Regardless of how their little wager turned out, Dalton would get to spend time with her. He almost hoped Sierra won because he'd love to have her all to himself at the swimming hole. Memories came rushing back. Her skin glistening like ivory in the pale moonlight, her red hair spilling down her back. The feel of her in his arms as the cool water lapped around them. The fire that raged through him when their lips connected. *Rein it in, boy*, he told himself. It was a simple walk. And while Sierra seemed different right this moment that didn't mean things would stay this way. There was still her life in New York and her hotshot boyfriend to consider.

She looked around, frowning. "I think I need to hire a landscaper to spruce this place up before the play. What do you think?"

He glanced around. "Yeah, it couldn't hurt. I could put you in touch with one of my guys."

Her eyes widened in surprise before an appreciative smile curved her lips. "Thanks."

The moment got slow as their eyes locked. Dalton was almost to his feet, about to pull her into her arms when she broke the connection. "Oh, I almost forgot. I need to snap a few pictures." Her words rushed out.

"Pictures?" He scratched his head. Sierra was squirrel jumping from topic to topic so fast it was hard to keep up.

She held up her phone. "Say cheese." She snapped the picture before he had a chance to smile. Then she turned and began taking pictures of the area.

"What's that for?"

"There. That should do it," she said to herself, then turned back to him as she shoved her phone in her back pocket. "I'm meeting with a few tourist companies tomorrow. Hopefully, they'll be able to sell some tickets." She paused. "We really need it."

The catch in her voice jumped out at him. "Need it for what?"

She blinked. "Huh?" She chuckled looking embarrassed. "Oh, it's nothing."

But he noticed the slight crease in her forehead, could tell by the way she held her mouth that something was wrong. He frowned. "What're you not telling me?"

"Nothing," she said with a half laugh. "*Geez.* You always take one little thing I say and blow it out of proportion."

Did he? Sierra had certainly accused him of that enough when they were together. He studied her. No, he wasn't off track. Something was wrong.

He rose to his feet. "Sie? What is it?" For an instant, the years turned back and he felt the same intense connection that had always been between them—as strong as the tide pulling the waves into the shore.

She offered a strained smile. "I could never keep anything from you." He was surprised to see tears glistening in her eyes. There was an expression on her face he couldn't decipher—pain, regret?

His voice went soft as he touched her arm. "What is it?" For a second, he thought she might refuse to answer but then her shoulders sagged.

"Bennie took out a loan against the mansion to fund this stupid theater." The vehemence in her voice cut like a blade through the moist air.

"What?" He'd always thought Bennie was smart with her money. This seemed out of character for her. Sure, she loved the theater and was a little eccentric, especially when she was getting into her roles. But putting herself in hock? Not something he would've expected.

"She's behind on her payments … twenty-two thousand dollars to be exact. If she doesn't get it caught up in the next few weeks, the bank will foreclose." Her voice trembled. "And we'll lose the mansion."

He shook his head. "Which bank is it?"

"The bank where Nadine works." She tucked a strand of hair behind her ear. "Anyway, that's why I came back." She motioned at the stage. "Why I'm getting involved in all this. And why I'm staying for the next four weeks."

Hope percolated in his chest. He loved hearing Sierra say out loud that she was staying four weeks. He stopped short when he saw tears brimming in her eyes. "Hey." He touched her arm. "It'll be all right."

She nodded, biting her lower lip.

It took everything in him to keep from pulling her into his arms. His heart was both broken and whole. She was here, right in front of him. And yet, she was no longer his. But still he craved her like a drowning man did air. If he pushed too hard, she'd run the other direction.

A slight smile touched her lips, then she let out an embarrassed laugh. "I'm sorry to burden you with my problems."

He shrugged. "No problem. That's what friends are for."

She cocked her head. "Is that what we are?"

"We were friends first, weren't we?" The friendship thing would work. Put her at ease.

Her eyes softened. "Yes, we were."

"'Friends at first, friends at last.' Isn't that how the saying goes?" Okay, that was a little much. A beat stretched between them as he sought for the right words to fill the silence.

"Yeah," she said quietly. Her eyes met his, and he saw a yearning that whispered to his soul. It gave him cause to hope that all wasn't lost between them. Anticipation tingled over his skin. They were at a crossroads. He could only hope and pray that things would sway in his favor. Otherwise, he was headed for major heartbreak. And he didn't know if his heart could handle it again. He motioned with his head. "Come on. Let's sit down. I believe it's time for the two of us to have a nice, long talk." Talking was good. Talking implied friendship … understanding, the two of them connecting on an emotional level, rather than the physical.

She looked hesitant at first pursing her lips together. Time seemed to stand still as she reached a decision. Finally, she nodded. "Yes, it's time."

CHAPTER 14

*N*othing's going to happen between me and Dalton. We're just talking. Old friends are allowed that privilege, right? And that's all we are. Friends.

Even as the thoughts flitted through her mind, Sierra knew they were lies. She'd come out here for the express purpose of finding Dalton, had even taken a shower and dressed in clothes she knew he'd like. Wore her hair super curly like he liked it.

Ever since her conversation with Nadine, she'd been in turmoil, had spent a solid hour pacing back and forth in her bedroom. If what Nadine said was true … about Dalton no longer drinking, then she'd made a huge mistake by leaving him. At first, she was so fighting mad at Nadine she could hardly see straight. Nadine had played a large part in her fleeing to New York. Heck, Nadine even gave her the money to get established. She'd trusted Nadine's judgment, believed her when she told Sierra she'd end up just like her mother if she stayed here with Dalton.

After the anger ran its course, Sierra realized she had to take responsibility for her own actions. She'd left because she wanted to go. She wanted to prove that she could make something of herself, and she'd been terrified of Dalton's drinking. Everything had come to a head that day she'd had the talk with Nadine. Sierra had been vulnerable, ready to act on whatever advice she was given. Especially from such a trusted source. But at the end of the day, she was accountable.

Finally, she decided that the best course of action was to face this. If her relationship with Parker was so weak that it couldn't withstand her spending a few weeks with Dalton, then that was her answer. But even if she chose Dalton, that didn't mean he'd choose her. They couldn't just erase the last seven years and pick up where they'd left off, could they? And what about her obligation to Parker? She'd built a relationship with him. Well, obviously not as strong of a relationship as she'd assumed. Otherwise, they'd already be engaged. But that was beside the point.

"Waffles."

She jerked slightly realizing Dalton was studying her. She gave him a courtesy smile. "Yeah, waffles." Being out here with Dalton unleashed so many memories that they rushed over her like a waterfall, making her have irrational thoughts. Thoughts like throwing caution to the wind and kissing him until her need for him was satisfied. No, that was the problem. She'd never get enough of Dalton Chandler. All he had to do was flash that leisurely grin and rove over her with those smoky eyes and she'd be reduced to a puddle of goo.

He angled to face her.

"So, what should we talk about?" she began, hoping he wouldn't bring up the topic of her leaving him. Then again, maybe it was better to get it out in the open rather than having it dangling over them. "What happened to your jaw?"

He looked surprised.

"The faint scar running along your jaw."

"Bar fight." He gave her a slight smile. "If you think this is bad, you should've seen the other guy."

"You always were a hothead." She assessed him. "When did you stop drinking?"

His eyes rounded. "You don't beat around the bush, do you?"

She clasped her hands tightly in her lap wanting to make herself small enough to be shielded from the ugliness of the past. "I figure it's easier to just rip off the Band-Aid in one fell swoop."

He gave her a curious look. "How did you know I stopped drinking?"

"Nadine told me."

"I didn't realize I'd been the hot topic of conversation," he said dryly.

"You have no idea," she muttered. "Is it true?" Her heart beat faster. "Are you sober?"

"Yeah, it's true." He looked puzzled and amused. "How about you?"

"Of course," she said impatiently. "I haven't touched a drop since I moved to New York. But I was never addicted like you were." She hated how pious her words sounded, but it was true. She could take or leave alcohol, whereas it had been Dalton's Achilles heel.

He blew out a heavy breath. "Yeah, I know." Remorse settled into his eyes. "I'm sorry for all the crap I put you through. It was a tough time with my dad. You know, trying to find out who I was."

Emotion thickened her throat as she swallowed, the memories of those terrible times overtaking her. "It was rough," she admitted. "I didn't have a clue how to deal with your destructive behavior."

He nodded, his jaw working. "I know. I'm sorry. My old man and I were volleying for power." He laughed humorlessly. "I was trying to show him that I was tougher than he was. If he was going to beat me, then by golly, he'd get beaten back."

"I remember." Dalton's dad would go into drunk rages and beat him. It had been happening since they were kids. Many a night, Dalton would sneak out of his house after his dad passed out and jog the half mile to the mansion. He'd climb up the trellis to the second story and in through her bedroom window. He'd sleep on a pallet beside her bed, just so he could be somewhere safe.

Her voice hitched, her hand clutching her neck. "That day when you insisted on driving … you were so drunk you could barely walk, much less drive. And then you took a curve too fast and we ended up in that field." She coughed, trying to stifle the quiver in her voice. "I thought we were goners. You missed that tree by only a few inches."

His face had gone the color of chalk, his lips drawn into a tight line. She could feel the regret emanating from him. "I went to Nadine's to see if Hal could pull us out because you were passed out cold from the booze." She hated rehashing all this. Hated all the emotion it unearthed. Hated the accusation in her voice, but wanting to set the stage. She needed him to understand her reasoning.

His brow furrowed, his eyes darkening to a fathomless gray. "The Camaro didn't get a scratch on it."

"I know," she said impatiently. "It's the *what could've happened* that got to me."

"I told you I was sorry and that it would never happen again."

"I wanted to believe you, truly. But I was afraid." Tears escaped the corners of her eyes and rolled down her cheeks. Hastily, she wiped them away with her palms.

A peculiar look came into his eyes. "Is that why you left? Because you were afraid I wouldn't stop drinking?"

"Partly."

He swore under his breath. Then he gulped out a laugh, bringing his hand to his mouth. "You know? Deep down, I think I knew that. Only I didn't really realize I knew it until just now." He ran a hand through his hair. "Wow. I lost you to the bottle. Ironic, isn't it? Considering my old man?"

"There's more." The air was so dense with moisture that Sierra knew the rain wouldn't hold off much longer. But she had to get this out, here and now. Otherwise, she'd never have the courage to bring it up again. She touched his arm. The pained look on his face clutched her stomach like a fist. "I was pregnant."

He gurgled, then coughed. "W-what?" His eyes bugged like his tongue was strangling his windpipe. "Why didn't you tell me?"

"I was afraid if I did, you might not leave for the Marines."

His brows bunched. "But I was only in basic training for a few weeks, then I was coming back to get you." Accusation brimmed in his eyes. "You knew that. Don't try to act like you didn't."

She hugged her arms. "Yeah, I guess you're right," she said flatly. "The truth is that I was terrified of ending up with an alcoholic. And then there was a baby to consider. We were so young. I didn't know what to do." Her voice trailed off.

A horrified look came over him. "Did you give the baby up for adoption?"

"No, I miscarried a week after you left."

He shook his head, a dazed look in his eyes. Then he raked both hands through his hair. "I still can't believe you didn't tell me." His voice broke. "Why couldn't you trust me?"

"I don't know." The words sounded empty and hollow. "Maybe it was myself that I couldn't trust." She let out a self-deprecating laugh. "I knew if I didn't leave you while you were gone, I'd never have the strength to leave you. I loved you so much. You were my world." She threw up her hands. "Heck, a part of me still loves you, even though heaven knows I've done everything I can to move past this."

"Do you have any idea what you put me through?" His eyes were harder than flint.

"It's not like you're the only one who was hurt," she flung back, heat spiking through her. She should've known better than to try and fix the past. "This is ridiculous," she muttered, jumping to her feet. She gritted her teeth, glaring at him. "I don't know why I bothered to come out here and try to explain this to you because you're never going to see anything other than your side of the story!"

He also stood, a fierce look in his eyes. "Don't walk away from me. We're not done here. Not by a long shot!"

She snorted out a laugh. "Oh, yes we are!" She felt first one raindrop then another. A second later, the bottom fell out, drenching them. She let out a shriek and was about to run back to the mansion, but he caught her arm, a hard smile stretching over his lips. "Looks like you won the wager. I guess we'll have to plan that walk."

"Yeah, I've changed my mind." There was something primal and raw about being out here with him in the rain, stripping away all pretense. His hair was pressed flat to his head, drawing attention to his rugged features. The wet t-shirt clung to his chiseled pecs and abs, his biceps as hard as granite. Attraction simmered through her, making her warm despite the cold.

He cocked an eyebrow. "You know what? All right. If that's the way you wanna play it. I changed my mind too. I'll take a kiss instead."

Her stomach flipped. "What?"

Before she could get away, he encircled her waist and pulled her close. The feel of his body against hers was overwhelming. Tingles burst through her when his lips came down on hers. She put up a half-second protest before the flame ignited. Seven years of wanting him was a long time, too long for her to deny him now. His lips were demanding as they licked fire through her toes, making her weak in the knees. He dipped her back as a groan escaped her throat. She ran her hands up his tapered back, burying her fingers in his hair. Delicious shivers circled down her spine as he intensified the kiss. A thrill of exhilaration shot through her and she had the sensation of soaring.

Parker had never kissed her like this, like he was drinking the last bit of her strength from her lips and then giving her back even more. She would've given up a thousand lifetimes for this kiss … a thousand lifetimes to be here in Dalton's arms. The feeling of love that poured through her was so swift that she thought her heart would burst.

When he released her lips, she tried to catch her breath, her hands resting on his rock-hard chest.

A satisfied smirk tugged at his lips.

"What?"

"I'll bet your boyfriend never kissed you like that."

She gasped like she'd been slapped. "Really? That's all you can say to me?" It then occurred to her that it was pouring buckets. A shiver ran through her. She was sure she had mascara trailing down her face. She tried to escape from his arms, but he held her in an iron grip. "Let me go," she seethed.

"For the record. I love you too."

"You're such a jerk," she said reflexively, then realized what he'd said. "Y-you do?" she sputtered.

He laughed. "Yes, I do."

She cocked her head. "But you said I'd done you a favor by leaving."

"I lied."

She frowned. "What?"

"You hurt me, so I wanted to hurt you."

"You're such a dork," she muttered. All that crap he said threw her for a loop, just as he knew it would.

He searched her face. "What now?"

She could tell from the intensity in his eyes that he was asking where they went from here. And truthfully, she didn't know. Could she leave New York and Parker and come back here? All her insecurities came flooding back with a vengeance. "I—I'm not sure." It was the most honest answer she could give him right now.

He seemed to be reading her mind as he frowned, a wounded look settling into his eyes. "Would you really leave me again?"

Everything was coming at her so fast she couldn't make sense of it all. "I have commitments in New York. A job. Parker." Oh, gosh. What would Parker think if he saw her now? Suddenly, she was ashamed of herself. Ashamed and confused.

His jaw went hard. "I see."

"I'm not saying I wouldn't stay here with you. I'm just saying I don't know right now." She hesitated. "Please, just give me a little time to sort this out, okay?"

His eyes narrowed. "Seven years isn't enough?"

"No ... I ..."

He dropped his arms. "You'd better get inside before you catch your death."

"Dalton ... please." A wave of panic rose in her chest, bringing tears to her eyes. "I'm just trying to be honest with you. All of this is too much for me right now, especially with Bennie's problems."

He nodded. "I understand."

But she could tell that he didn't.

He motioned with his head. "Go on in. I've got to get my tools out of this rain before they get ruined." His voice sounded as flat and dead as she felt.

"I'll help."

"No!"

She flinched at the hard edge in his voice.

He held up a hand. "I'll take care of it. Just go. Please."

She cringed at the desperation in his voice. A curious numbness came over her. "Okay." Her voice sounded small and insignificant in her ears as she turned and trudged back to the mansion, her tears mixing with the rain.

CHAPTER 15

"You know, it'd be so much easier if you'd just swallow your pride and go talk to Dalton." Bennie shook her head remorsefully. "I can't stand to see you moping around. You've been like this for days."

Sierra ground her teeth together, her eyes narrowing to slits. "I have not been moping around." She drew herself up. "I'll have you know, I'm perfectly fine." She wasn't fine. She hadn't slept well in days, and she kept replaying that kiss—could still feel the burn from it on her lips, could still smell Dalton's clean masculine scent with a hint of musk and mint.

Bennie let out a long sigh. "Well, you certainly don't look fine." She was sitting at the kitchen table playing Solitaire. Sierra was at the sink loading the dishes from breakfast into the dishwasher. It had been a week and a day since she and Dalton had kissed and then everything fell apart. She'd not seen hide nor hair of him since.

According to Bennie, he'd been coming every evening to work on the set, but Sierra wasn't about to go out there. If Dalton Chandler wanted to talk, he knew where to find her. She still couldn't believe he'd pushed her away like that, just because she wasn't ready that instant to flush her life and career down the drain and put down roots in Sugar Pines. He was an egotistical jerk who was way too good looking for his own good. Well, she hoped he had a long and happy life with Ivie Jane Compton. Her insides shriveled at the thought.

"Your foolish pride's gonna be the death of you."

She threw down the dish towel and spun around. "What?" An unreasonable anger seized her. "My foolish pride?" She belted out a hard laugh. "I'm not the one who put the mansion in jeopardy to finance a stupid theater."

Bennie pulled the tie on her robe tighter, her eyes sparking. "You're out of line."

A raucous laugh scratched Sierra's throat. "Seriously? Do you know what a difficult situation you've put us in?" Her voice rose. "Do you? I've tried everything I can think of to boost ticket sales for the second round of performances and we're only at thirty percent capacity." Her voice went shrill. "Do you know what that means, Bennie?"

Her jaw went slack. "I thought you'd worked out something with the tourist companies."

"Yeah, one gave me the brush-off. One sounded fairly interested, and the third is on board ... six months from now. That's how far in advance they book their events."

"Why didn't you tell me?"

A deep weariness settled over Sierra as she folded her arms over her chest. "I don't know. I guess I didn't want to cause you anymore stress." She looked at Bennie's knee. "And have you end up in the hospital again."

Bennie let out a long sigh. "You know what? You should stop worrying about the mansion and take some time for yourself. Go shopping for a dress to wear tonight at Boyd Compton's party."

An incredulous laugh rose in Sierra's throat. Had she really just heard her aunt correctly? "I have to worry about the mansion. Otherwise, we'll lose it."

"It'll work out. You'll see. I'll make an appointment with Leo Farnsworth at the bank the first of next week. I'm sure the two of us can work something out."

Sierra's hand flew to her hip. "Well, according to Nadine, unless you can produce twenty-two thousand dollars, the bank's going to foreclose."

She clucked her tongue. "Nadine's a worry wart. She's exaggerating."

"And you're like an ostrich, burying your head in the sand. But it won't work this time, Bennie. You can't just close your eyes and hope the problem will go away. We have to face it."

"Yes, you're right. That's why I'll go and talk to Leo next week. Okay?"

Sierra blew out a breath. "Okay." She and Bennie ripping each other apart wasn't going to solve anything.

Bennie's eyes lit up. "All right it's settled then."

"What's settled?" Sierra smelled a trap.

"You're going to get something nice to wear for Boyd Compton's party tonight. Oh, and while you're out, maybe you could pick up some milk and bread. And ham and cheese."

A sense of horror trickled down her spine. "I'm not going to that party," she spat. The thought of being there with Dalton and Ivie Jane churned her gut sour.

Bennie peered over her glasses. "I promised Dalton and Boyd that I'd be there tonight." She punched the table with her finger, enunciating every word. "And I can't go alone."

Sierra felt the noose closing in around her as she touched her neck. "What about Nadine and Hal? Can't they take you?"

"Nope. They're having their kids and grandkids over for dinner tonight."

She waved her hand. "Well, what about Wesley? Can't he take you?"

"He has to work tonight." She flashed a checkmate smile. "So, it's you and me, kiddo. Are you going shopping?"

"No, I'm not," she huffed. She might be getting roped into going to the stupid party, but she was drawing the line at going shopping for it.

Bennie's eyebrows went down in a V. "Well, what're you wearing then?"

"Something that I already have." *Geez Louise.* The woman could pester the horns off a goat.

"What?" Bennie pressed.

"A dress." Her voice took on a spiteful edge. "Don't worry. It'll be something nice. I won't embarrass you."

"We'll see." Bennie rolled her eyes.

Sierra's phone buzzed. She reached in her pocket to retrieve it. Parker. Was he calling about work? No, that wasn't it. Everything was on schedule for the Pristine Pizza account. Ross Snyder, the owner, went gaga over the old-fashioned soda shop idea. All was good with the team. This had to be a personal call. She'd been dodging Parker's calls all week. And when she couldn't avoid talking to him, she'd kept the conversation short and relegated to surface items. She was sure Parker knew that something was wrong, but it would have to ride for a while because she wasn't ready to talk to him yet. First, she had to get this thing with Dalton sorted through.

It was scary how much Dalton dominated her thoughts the past week. And what was even worse, she actually missed him. How was that even possible? Was she losing her mind? Probably. Yesterday, she'd called Harley, her best friend from Camp Wallakee. She'd hoped the conversation would help her get back on track, but it did just the opposite. Harley was falling for some cowboy, the antithesis of a Jane Austen hero. It was like Harley was throwing everything they'd planned and worked for right out the window. And Harley even had the audacity to suggest that Sierra give Dalton a second chance. Had the whole world gone nuts?

Yes, it had gone nuts ... including her, because she was thinking of taking Harley's advice. Despite her best efforts to steer away from Dalton, all roads kept leading back to him. Heaven help her!

Bennie put down her cards. "Have a seat."

For a second Sierra thought about refusing, but then sighed irritably as she pulled out a chair and slumped down.

Bennie looked her in the eye. "Okay, it's time for the two of us to talk turkey."

Uh, oh. She didn't know if she was up to having a heart-to-heart with Bennie. She felt haggard and defeated and so dang unsure about everything. Before coming home, everything was clicking. Sure, she was disappointed that Parker didn't propose, but it would come ... eventually. She scrunched her brows. At this point, she wasn't sure that she even wanted Parker to propose.

"How are you doing?"

The tenderness in Bennie's voice brought tears to Sierra's eyes. She hiccuped a laugh. "Not too good," she admitted.

Bennie nodded. Then she took a deep breath, her lips forming a straight line. "I'm going to ask you a simple question, and I want you to give me a truthful answer."

"Okay," she said wariness trickling over her.

"Are you still in love with Dalton?"

She laughed in surprise, balling her fist. "What?"

Bennie sat back and folded her arms over her chest, eyeing her.

Her mind ran through a dozen answers, creative ways to dodge the question. But then she experienced a blip of clarity. Just like that, Bennie had pulled away the superfluous and gotten to the root of the problem. "Yes," she heard herself say. It was actually a relief to admit it out loud. Her pulse cranked up a notch. She was in love with him now as much as she'd ever been. All the time apart, the goals she'd set for herself, the Jane Austen Pact, her bright future in New York ... None of it could withstand a handful of days with Dalton.

"He loves you. You love him. What's the problem?"

"Well, for starters, he's a jerk!" She bunched her eyebrows together, the anger resurfacing. "He doesn't understand that I might need a few days to shift gears before throwing my life away."

Bennie cocked her head. "Is that what you think? That you'd be throwing your life away by staying here and choosing Dalton?"

Crap! Every time she turned around she was offending someone. She pulled at the collar of her t-shirt. "I'm not trying to come across as a snot," she mumbled. "Only trying to express how I feel." If she couldn't say these things to Bennie, then who could she tell?

A tiny smile curved Bennie's lips. "Believe it or not, I totally get where you're coming from."

She jerked, her eyes going to Bennie's. "You do?"

"Yeah." She laughed dryly. "I know it's hard to believe from looking at me now, but I was young once. I always dreamed of going to New York and performing on Broadway."

"Why didn't you?" The answer came the instant she voiced the question. "It was because of me, wasn't it?" A pit settled in her stomach. Bennie got saddled with a twelve-year-old kid to raise. Of course she couldn't go anywhere. She'd been stuck here her entire life. No wonder she was determined to put on those plays, build her outdoor theater. As she looked across the table at her aging aunt, it hit her that Bennie was still a beautiful woman with her silver hair, bright eyes, and porcelain skin. All in all, the two of them really weren't that different.

Bennie reached across the table for Sierra's hand, her eyes going moist. "Raising you has been the greatest blessing of my life."

Tears brimmed in Sierra's eyes. "Really?"

"Really. You're my daughter, and I love you with my whole heart. I want you to be happy. You have a good man who loves you, and you love him."

Could she and Dalton make it work? The notion sent hope rising in her breast. But could she give up her career? Then again, she wouldn't have to. There were advertising agencies in Charleston. Eventually, she could start her own agency, if she wanted.

Bennie quirked a smile as she removed her hand from Sierra's. "That little mind's going a mile a minute. What're you thinking about?"

A grin spilled over her lips. "I was thinking that you're a wonderful aunt … mother." The word landed softly on her lips, a proclamation of the heart. "Thank you."

"No thanks necessary, love. That's what mom's do." A tear rolled down her cheek as she laughed and swiped it away like it was a pesky insect. "Okay, enough of the mushy stuff. What're you going to do about Dalton?"

"I'm not sure." Her mouth tightened. "I'm still ticked at him."

Bennie chuckled. "The more things change …"

"The more they stay the same," Sierra finished with a laugh. She and Dalton had always fought and loved hard. He was so intense that fighting was often the only thing he understood.

"I've got one more bit of advice," Bennie said, looking thoughtful.

"Okay."

"You've had some hard knocks, gone through things that no person should ever have to experience. But it has made you strong. Much stronger than you realize."

Was she strong? She didn't feel strong.

"Life is giving you another chance to find real happiness. Not the New York version that comes wrapped in a fancy bow with a hefty price tag. But lasting happiness with a man you've loved since practically birth."

She gulped, trying to swallow back the tidal wave of emotion rising in her throat.

A smile played on Bennie's lips, her voice growing practical. "Here's how I see it. You're beautiful ..." her eyes twinkled "... somewhat intelligent, part of the time."

"Hey," Sierra countered.

Bennie laughed. "The point is, dear, that you've got the world at your feet. And even better, you're not married to Parker or even engaged. You have the wonderful ability to do what you want. The choice is yours." Her eyes burned into Sierra's as she leaned forward. "Sierra McCain. The question that you need to ask yourself is this ... What is it that you truly want?"

CHAPTER 16

*D*alton wasn't proud of the way he'd handled himself with Sierra. Things had been going better than he could've ever hoped, and then he panicked when she told him she needed time to sort through her feelings. And he'd pushed her away. In his defense, she'd leveled some pretty hard blows. He couldn't believe she'd gotten pregnant and had a miscarriage. She'd gone through it all on her own because she couldn't depend on him.

Now that he'd had time to think things through, he understood where Sierra was coming from. He'd been a wreck back then, always making empty promises that he'd quit drinking. Had he not joined the Marines and met Randal Murphy he probably would've ended up a drunk like his old man.

His dad died a couple of years ago from liver cancer brought on by the drinking. And while they had a form of a reconciliation, there was no way his dad could make up for all the damage he'd caused. Despite it all, Dalton still missed him. He was his dad, after all.

Dalton's thoughts went back to Randal, his heart clutching the way it always did when he thought of his close friend, who'd been killed when a Harrier went down. They'd met during his first year of service. Randal was older than most Marines, in his early thirties.

After Dalton realized Sierra had left him, he was in a dark place, had even contemplated suicide. While he didn't know if he would've ever gone through with it, he was still headed down a destructive path—hanging out at bars, drinking himself into oblivion.

Randal had taken him under his wing and introduced him to religion. Prayer was what ultimately saved Dalton. With God's help, he found the strength to overcome his addiction. Once Dalton got himself straightened out and off the booze, Randal taught him how to trade stocks, a skill that benefitted him to this day. Sierra would be shocked if she knew how much he was worth. He couldn't help but smile a little at that.

He pulled into the circular driveway of the Compton's large, colonial home and turned off the engine. There were already dozens of cars and people filing in through the front door. Dalton adjusted his necktie and checked his reflection in the mirror, smoothing a hand over his hair. He wasn't looking forward to this party tonight. While he could hold his own in large social situations, they really weren't his thing.

What he wanted most was to find Sierra and kiss her again. Then he'd apologize for his hasty reaction. Of course, it still bothered him that Sierra would actually consider going back to New York. His stomach knotted. Would he lose her all over again? He sucked in a breath, willing himself to focus on the positive as he got out of his Camaro. He drove it tonight because his truck was in the shop getting repaired.

Music floated on the evening air from the live band. The party was being held out back by the Olympic-sized pool and clubhouse. The scent of food teased his senses, but Dalton couldn't distinguish the type of food. He knew whatever it was would be tasty because Janie's restaurant was catering the party. A slight breeze ruffled his hair. Janie had a knack for obsessing over details and she freaked out when she learned there was a chance of rain in the forecast. Her fears were in vain because the weather was perfect.

He dreaded talking to Janie. He knew now that he couldn't continue his relationship with her. Not when he was so over the moon for Sierra. Regardless of what happened between him and Sierra, it wouldn't be fair to string Janie along.

He smiled and nodded at the familiar faces as he adjusted his sports coat and strode up the wide steps. Would Sierra be here tonight? He'd spoken to Bennie earlier in the day, and she assured him that Sierra was coming. But Dalton wasn't certain. He was sure she was still furious at him.

He walked through the house and out the double French doors. The area was brimming with people holding drinks in their hands. A young server wearing a uniform approached, flashing a cheery smile. "Can I get you a drink, sir?"

"Yes, a club soda with lime please."

She nodded. "I'll be right back."

It used to bother Dalton to be around alcohol, but now he didn't think twice about it. Ironically, the only time he'd even thought about drinking the past few years was the day Sierra came back to town. Yep, she was his weakness, even greater than alcohol.

The server returned with the club soda. "Thanks," he said, taking a sip. He scoured the crowd, searching for Sierra. Disappointment settled over him when he didn't see her. But it was still early. He spotted Janie near the band, laughing and talking to a group of friends. When she saw him, she gave him a big smile and wave. Then she came over to him. "Hey, babe. You look fantastic."

"Thanks. So do you." It was true. By all definitions, she was stunning in her bright yellow dress that hugged her curves. She was great … for some other guy. She went to kiss him on the lips, he turned so that she got his cheek instead.

She gave him a funny look. "Everything okay?"

He forced a smile. "Great."

She took his arm. "Come on. I wanna introduce you to a few people."

He groaned inwardly. And so it began—the hour or so of polite conversation.

~

SIERRA'S NERVES were jumping like a squirrel on caffeine as she got out of the car and went around to the passenger side to help Bennie out. The last time she'd stepped foot in this house, she and Ivie Jane had been best friends. That was before she became the town pariah. The thought left a sour taste in her mouth. She held out her hand and helped Bennie to her feet. Bennie used the hood of the car for support while Sierra handed her the crutches. It took some effort for Bennie to get them under her arms balancing on one foot.

"Are you sure this is a good idea? I don't want you to fall and break your neck. Maybe we should just go back home." Coming back here, being around all these people from her youth, wasn't sitting well. She could always talk to Dalton another time.

"I'll be fine." Bennie smiled reassuringly. "I'm a lot tougher than I look."

"Yeah, I know. You're a tough old bird. But don't get overconfident." She looked down at the uneven cobblestones. "Especially around these."

"I've got it."

Sierra stayed close to Bennie, ready to catch her at any second should she trip.

Once inside on a smooth surface, it was easier for Bennie to walk. As soon as they stepped through the doors leading to outside, Sierra searched for an empty table. "Over there." She pointed as they made their way over to it. She pulled out a chair and helped Bennie get seated.

Sierra was relieved when Bennie got situated and propped her crutches against the table. A grin tugged at her lips. "You're a lot of work," she teased.

Bennie laughed. "That's what they tell me." Her breathing was labored from the exertion, and she wiped her forehead. Then she fluffed her hair and straightened her glasses. "Now," she sighed, settling into the chair.

Sierra was about to sit down, but Bennie made a shooing motion. "You need to go mingle." Bennie grinned like a Cheshire cat. "Go find your man."

Nervous butterflies thrummed in Sierra's stomach. Dalton was here with Ivie Jane. She couldn't just burst in between them and say *pick me*. She chuckled inwardly at the thought. That would give the good townsfolk of Sugar Pines something to talk about.

Someone touched her arm. For one wild second, Sierra thought it was Dalton but was surprised to see Boyd Compton standing before her. He was the picture of refinement with his graying temples and patrician features.

"Good evening," he said, offering a formal bow.

"Hello. Happy birthday," Sierra blurted.

"Thank you." He acknowledged Bennie with a nod, which she returned with a regal nod of her own. If Sierra didn't know better, she'd think Bennie was a queen nodding to her subject. Sierra bit back a smile. Bennie really was a great actress.

Boyd rocked on his heels and cleared his throat. "Might I have a word with you?"

Her throat tightened. "Uh, yeah. Sure." She glanced at Bennie who looked as surprised as she. Boyd directed her over to a private area beside a row of tall hedges.

Sierra's mind whirled. What in the world could the man want to tell her? Even when she and Ivie Jane were friends he'd been aloof, only marginally polite. She'd always thought of him as a stuffed shirt.

"There's no easy way to say this," he said stiffly.

Was he going to warn her to stay away from Dalton?

"Young lady, I owe you an apology."

Her jaw dropped. "Excuse me?"

A twinge of pain touched his dark eyes. "When Loretta was killed in the accident, I was a broken man."

A shudder went through Sierra, making her knees go weak. Was he really bringing up her mother's car wreck?

The corners of his jaw twitched, and Sierra could tell it was an effort to get out whatever it was he was trying to say. "I was so consumed with grief that I only thought of myself and Ivie Jane." His voice caught as he looked at her, remorse simmering in his eyes. "I should've stopped to realize that we weren't the only ones who lost a loved one that day."

Without warning, tears rushed to her eyes as she blinked.

"I can't imagine how hard it must've been for you. Not only to lose your mother, but to have Ivie Jane and your friends turn against you."

"Yes, it was," Sierra said quietly. For so long she'd carried the guilt of what her mother had done, even though she had no control over it.

"I'm sorry," he said gruffly.

Sierra couldn't stop the tears from spilling over her cheeks. An unexpected warmth flowed into her, like the sun giving light to a cloudy day. She smiled at Boyd. "Thank you. I know it wasn't easy for you to tell me that."

He nodded and glanced around like he didn't know what else to say. "Well, have a good evening."

"You too."

He turned on his heel and strode back to the crowd.

When she returned to the table, Bennie lifted an eyebrow. "What did he want?"

"I think in his own way, he was apologizing for allowing Ivie Jane and her buddies to oust me."

She grunted. "About time. That's what he should've done years ago instead of showing up at the door with a wad of cash to send you to Camp Wallakee. The old fart wanted to ease his conscience."

Sierra's eyes bulged. "What? Boyd paid for that? You told me you'd put aside extra money from your music lessons to pay for it."

Bennie's mouth formed an O. "Did I say that?"

"Yes, you did." The situation struck Sierra as funny as a laugh rumbled in her throat. "Bennie, Bennie. What am I gonna do with you?"

"Well, if you haven't figured it out by now, you probably never will," she responded tartly.

"True," Sierra agreed.

"Sierra."

She turned toward the high-pitched voice and saw Dalton's assistant, Phyllis Watson and Eddie Whitehead standing beside the food table. Phyllis's hand flapped back and forth as she waved wildly. "Come over here."

"Oh, no," Bennie said dryly. "That motor-mouth'll monopolize you all night if you let her."

Sierra laughed. "Yeah, probably. I guess I'd better go say *hello*."

"Careful," Bennie warned. "Whatever you say can and will be used against you and then spread all over Sugar Pines."

Sierra chuckled, knowing Bennie was right. She smoothed down her dress and pasted on her best debutante smile.

"Hey," Phyllis chirped, giving her a tight hug. She looked Sierra up and down. "Wow! That's some dress." She nudged Eddie. "Doesn't she look pretty?"

"Yeah," he said dutifully.

Sierra looked down at her emerald dress, the same one she and Juliette had picked out from the boutique the day she thought Parker would propose. "Thanks," she smiled.

"How ya doin', Sierra?" Eddie drawled, using his two front teeth to lob off the top section of the chicken on a skewer.

"Good, Eddie. How are you?"

He shook his head. A smile eased over his lips as he talked with his mouth full. "Still sorry I had to give such a pretty little thing like you a ticket."

Phyllis's face scrunched as she hit his arm. "I'm right here, Bozo."

His eyes bugged, and for a second it looked like he might be choking. He let out a forceful cough. "You're the one who said she was pretty. I was just going along with it."

"Well, okay, if that's all it is," Phyllis said stiffly, adjusting her dress. Eddie put an arm around Phyllis, winking at Sierra.

"My woman here gets a little jealous, because she loves me so much."

Sierra laughed. "I can see that."

"Yeah, I do love ya. But that still doesn't mean I don't wanna wring your skinny neck sometimes." Phyllis smiled brightly at Sierra. "Did I tell you we're engaged?" She held up her finger and wiggled it, just as she'd done the first day Sierra got to town.

"Yes, you told me."

Phyllis made a face. "Oh, yeah. That's right. I forgot."

It was then that Sierra realized Dalton was striding towards them. There was something so magnetic about his presence that she couldn't take her eyes off him. Her heart started racing. He wore a blue tie, matching sports coat, and khaki pants. His hair was messy, a strand hanging over one eye, giving him a bad-boy look. As unobtrusively as she could, she sucked in a breath, trying to appear somewhat composed.

"Hey, Sie," he drawled, a slow smile flowing over his lips.

"Hey." A heat wave blasted over her, and she knew her face was blaring like a sunburn. She probably should've acted more put out since he'd ignored her all week, but all she could think about was that he was here ... talking to her! Boyd apologizing, Dalton here, the music flowing, the twinkling white lights. She was starting to feel like she was in a fairy tale.

Dalton's eyes moved over her like a caress. "You look incredible," he murmured. He touched her arm, leaning in to give her a kiss on the cheek. Her skin tingled wildly under his touch, and she caught the spice of his cologne mingled with his scent—fresh and masculine like the ocean that had been their playground. The past and present melded together into a powerful punch. She caught the longing in his eyes, knew the same vibe was reflecting off her. Then there was a whisper of something as ageless as the velvety sky above them.

Dalton belonged to her, as she did to him. And wherever he was ... that's where her home would be.

"Hey, old man," Eddie said. "Looking good." He gnawed off another piece of chicken.

"Thanks," Dalton uttered, not taking his eyes off Sierra. "We need to talk."

"Yes," she said simply.

Ivie Jane's ultra-cheery voice over the microphone broke the spell. "Ladies and gentlemen, thanks so much for coming out tonight to celebrate Daddy's birthday."

Sierra jumped slightly turning toward the stage. She glanced at Dalton whose features tightened.

Ivie motioned at Boyd who was standing near the stage. "Give it up, folks, for my wonderful daddy who turned sixty-four today."

Boyd smiled and waved at the crowd. He seemed uncomfortable with the attention, but was gracious about it.

"Now, I've got a surprise for you," Ivie Jane said, her voice juicy. "My boyfriend Dalton Chandler's going to perform a song for you."

The crowd went wild.

For an instant, Sierra felt like she'd been slapped. She'd gotten so caught up in her own head about Dalton that she forgot for a moment that he was Ivie Jane's boyfriend. She looked at Dalton who had a thunderous look on his face. It was obvious the announcement came as a surprise.

"Dalton, come on up here," Ivie Jane said.

Dalton's eyes connected with Sierra's. "I still wanna have that talk."

"Yeah," she said dully. "Better go on up. You're being summoned by your girlfriend." She didn't try to hide the bite in her voice. She realized with a jolt that Phyllis was watching her, an amused expression on her face.

Sierra forced a smile. "It was great seeing you both. Excuse me." She hurried back to Bennie's table. The last thing she wanted was for Phyllis to be standing there assessing her like some science project while Dalton sang.

CHAPTER 17

"*Y*ou didn't tell me you were gonna have me sing." Dalton muttered as Janie thrust him a guitar.

She smiled, but her eyes flashed with anger. "I had to do something to get you away from Sierra," she hissed. "You're like a moth to the flame."

He'd intended to wait until after Boyd's birthday party to drop the bomb on Janie, but he knew it couldn't wait. "I'm sorry, Ivie," he said quietly, his eyes conveying all that his lips didn't have time to say right now.

Her face crumbled slightly. "So now I'm Ivie instead of Janie? *Figures!*" She plastered on a hard smile. "Break a leg," she barked.

He put the guitar strap over his shoulder and faced the crowd, his trademark smile slipping over his lips. "Howdy, folks," he boomed. "How y'all doing tonight?"

Thunderous applause sounded through the crowd.

The familiar comfort of the stage settled over Dalton like a favorite pair of faded jeans. He'd caught the stricken look on Sierra's face when Ivie Jane announced that he was her boyfriend. That hadn't scored him any brownie points with Sierra, that was for sure. He looked over to where she'd been standing, but with the lights, he couldn't see anything. His heart dropped. Hopefully, she hadn't left. For a second there, when they'd looked at each other, he got the distinct impression that she'd come back to him. And then Ivie Jane pulled this stunt and quite possibly ruined everything.

What was he going to sing? His mind ran through his list of usual songs. A smile slid over his lips. He knew exactly what he needed to do to get Sierra back. He stepped up to the microphone. "I wrote this one for my best friend. It's called *The One I'll Never Forget*."

SIERRA HAD JUST REACHED Bennie's table and was about to demand that they leave this instant when she heard the title of the song. She stopped in her tracks, turning toward the stage. Dalton's tenor voice rang out clear, jolting her to the core. She knew the lyrics to this song as well as she knew her own heartbeat. It was the song he wrote for her.

I saw you standing by the sea, copper curls blowing in the wind.
And I told my heart to be still because you were just a friend.

But with our friendship began a love that will never end.

All my love to you I send.

Baby, I need you like the earth needs the rain. You hold my heart in your hand.

I love you more than the ocean, sky, and sand.

And I just want you to understand.

You're my best friend. The one I'll never forget.

As the last note of the song faded away, Sierra let the tears fall unabashedly down her cheeks. A sigh escaped her mouth, her hand going over her heart. She looked at Bennie who also had tears streaming down her face.

The next second, pandemonium broke out when Ivie Jane stomped onto the stage and slapped Dalton across the jaw, the microphone amplifying the loud whack. Murmurs rippled through the crowd. "I hate you," Ivie Jane cried. "Curse you and curse Sierra for coming back here!" She erupted into tears and ran off the stage.

Sierra went stone cold as all eyes turned to her. Then came the sting of embarrassment. She just stood there, frozen. She felt someone touch her arm and realized Bennie was beside her.

"Let's get out of here before they tar and feather us," Bennie said, hobbling forward on her crutches, Sierra hurrying behind.

IN RETROSPECT, it probably wasn't the smartest idea to sing that song, but Dalton was so desperate to get Sierra back. And Ivie had goaded him into it. But she'd gotten her revenge, humiliated him and Sierra in front of the town. A hysterical laugh escaped his throat. He didn't care about the embarrassment. His only thought was to find Sierra.

He removed the guitar strap and hurried down the steps. He rushed back to where Phyllis and Eddie were standing. "Where is she?"

Eddie scratched his head. "She left, man, with her aunt. Right after your song."

His heart dropped. Was Sierra okay that he sang that song? He had to get to her. He was almost to the double French doors when someone stopped him.

"Dalton?"

He didn't want to talk to anyone right now, but decorum demanded that he pause and at least be polite. "Huh?" Then he realized it was Leo Farnsworth, the president of the bank that was about to foreclose on Bennie's mansion.

Leo cleared his throat. "That was an interesting song. And then afterwards …" He chugged out a few laughs. "Well, I thought I had problems with my wife, but well, yours take the cake."

"O-kay." He rubbed his jaw, not sure how else to respond.

Leo's thin mustache twitched as he cleared his throat. "Anyway, the reason I stopped you is because my assistant Nadine said you called to make an appointment and that it was extremely urgent." He searched Dalton's face. "I'm headed to Orlando next week on vacation, so I thought I'd better catch you tonight. Is everything okay?"

Dalton ran a hand through his hair. "Yeah, I do want to talk to you." He motioned. "Could you step inside for a minute, so we can speak in private?"

"Certainly." Leo straightened his jacket as he followed Dalton into the home.

"I wanted to talk to you about Bennie McCain's loan. I'd like to cover the balance."

He hesitated. "I don't understand. Does Bennie want to take out a loan? Are you planning on co-signing with her?"

"No, I want to talk to you about the loan she already has … the one she's behind on."

"Um … there must be some mistake."

"The loan against the mansion," Dalton said, feeling like he was stating the obvious.

Leo's forehead wrinkled. "Bennie doesn't have a loan through my bank."

Dalton frowned. "Are you sure?" He could've sworn that Sierra told him it was Leo's bank. Yes, she'd said it was the bank where Nadine worked. "So you're telling me that Bennie McCain doesn't owe your bank twenty-two thousand dollars and that you're not about to foreclose on her mansion?"

Leo gurgled out a nervous laugh. "That's exactly what I'm telling you. Bennie McCain doesn't have a loan with my bank."

"You're sure?"

"Absolutely." He lifted his chin. "I know all the ins and outs of my bank. I don't know where you're getting your information, but I can assure you it's false."

"Okay, thanks. If you'll excuse me." He hurried to his car.

Something was fishy about this whole thing. And he was going to find out what, as soon as he could get to Bennie's mansion.

CHAPTER 18

The minute Sierra and Bennie got in the door, Nadine burst in.

"I heard about the blowup at Boyd's party." She looked wide-eyed at Sierra. "Are you okay?"

"Yeah, I'm okay," Sierra answered and realized she really was. In fact, she was more than okay. But she needed to see Dalton. Would he stop by here? Maybe she should call him. She didn't even have his number, but Bennie did.

Nadine sat down on the couch beside Bennie, her eyes gleaming with interest. "Did Ivie Jane really slap Dalton and tell him off after he sang the song about Sierra?"

"Yep." Bennie chuckled. "It was quite the spectacle. I'm sure tongues will be wagging about that for a long time." She gave Sierra an apologetic look. "Sorry, but it's true."

Sierra sat down. "Yeah, you're probably right." She was trying to figure out a diplomatic way to ask Bennie for Dalton's number when the doorbell rang. She jumped back up and went to answer it. Her heart leapt in her mouth when she realized it was Dalton. "Hey," she said, heat flowing through her.

"Hey." He didn't wait to be invited, but stepped into the foyer.

Then she got a good look at his expression, her stomach tightening. Dalton was worried ... furious. Surely he wasn't this upset about Ivie Jane. He had to have known she would freak out when he sang that song. "What's wrong?"

He looked past her to the parlor where Bennie and Nadine were sitting. His eyes hardened as he grabbed Sierra's hand. "Come on. We need some answers."

"What answers?" she asked dubiously, noticing how his hand felt over hers. *Wow.* The attraction she felt to this man was incredible. She forced her mind to concentrate on the events taking place.

"Hey, Dalton." Bennie let out a string of chuckles that rumbled in her chest. "That was some performance."

"Yeah," Nadine piped in with a coy smile. "It sounds like you brought down the house."

Sierra saw Bennie and Nadine's eyes zoom in on her and Dalton's clasped hands. Bennie's expression radiated triumph as she clutched Nadine's arm. Nadine, too, was beaming. Something strange was going on here. It was like Bennie and Nadine were sharing a victory.

"Have a seat," Bennie said, motioning to the loveseat.

"We'll stand, thanks," Dalton said curtly. Sierra gave him a questioning look. It wasn't like Dalton to be rude to Bennie. But he was openly glaring at her like he was livid about something.

"I had a nice chat with Leo Farnsworth tonight about your bank loan." Accusation dripped from Dalton's mouth.

Sierra turned to him. "You what?" She looked at Bennie and Nadine whose faces had gone ghostly white.

"Yes, I offered to pay off the loan," Dalton said.

Tears pooled in Sierra's eyes. "You what?" A rush of tenderness welled in her chest as she turned to face this complex, frustrating, wonderful man who'd stolen her heart long ago and never gave it back. "I can't believe you'd do that for me."

His eyes went soft. "I'd do anything for you, Sie. You know that."

She nodded. Then a thought struck her. "But how? How did you get that kind of money?"

He gave her a half smile. "As it turns out, I'm not half bad at trading stocks."

She let out a soft gasp. "That's how you got the money to buy the Drexel Mansion," she mused.

A hint of amusement sparked in his eyes. "Don't look so shocked."

She shook her head, trying to take it all in. Then a sense of exultation rippled through her as she laughed. They wouldn't lose the mansion. "Thank you," she breathed. She lifted her lips and planted a kiss on his lips, electricity zinging through her.

He frowned. "Don't thank me yet."

Her face fell. "What do you mean?"

He eyed Bennie. "There was no loan."

Sierra wasn't sure she'd heard him correctly. "What?"

"There was no loan," he repeated.

Sierra's mind began to spin. "But that's impossible." The breath whooshed out of her lungs, her heart thudding dully like a deflated ball. She looked at Bennie and Nadine who seemed like they might pass out any minute. Her knees went weak. She needed to sit down. She released Dalton's hand and fell back into the loveseat. Dalton sat down beside her. "I don't understand." She looked at Bennie, who gave her a sheepish grin.

"There was no loan?" Her mind clicked through the events that had sent her racing home to save the mansion. Her telling Bennie over the phone that Parker was proposing. Nadine calling later that night to tell her about Bennie's accident and the impending foreclosure. Anger coursed through her veins and pumped to her temples with such force that she felt like her head would explode. She gave Bennie a withering look. "Is your knee really injured? Is it?" she screamed. Dalton put a calming hand on her arm.

"No," Bennie said, her voice sounding small.

Sierra swore under her breath. A harsh laugh scratched her throat. "This whole thing was a setup? You writhing in pain. The Emergency Room. The doctor. Was it all a sham?"

Bennie shrugged, a sheepish expression on her face. "'All the world's a stage, and all the men and women merely players—"

156

"Save it!" Fire blazed through Sierra, making her dizzy. She turned to Dalton. "They set us up."

His eyes widened, then narrowed as he glared at Bennie and Nadine. "How could you toy with our lives like this?" He shook his head. "Sierra's been worried sick about the mansion."

Tears burned Sierra's eyes. "How could you do this?" she demanded, looking at Bennie.

Nadine held up a hand. "It was my idea."

"Don't," Bennie said.

Nadine touched Bennie's arm. "But it's true."

Sierra had the feeling that they'd stepped into some crazy realm where everything was turned upside down. "This whole thing was your idea? But why?"

Nadine sighed heavily, locking eyes with Sierra. "It all goes back to the conversation we had that day when Hal pulled you out of the field."

Dalton bunched his brows. "Are you talking about the accident we had right before I went into the Marines?"

Nadine nodded.

He let out an incredulous laugh. "This is insane." He turned to Sierra, a wild look in his eyes. "They've lost their minds."

"Not hardly," Bennie said dryly. "Just hear Nadine out."

Nadine continued her narrative. "When Hal and I arrived at the field ..." she eyed Dalton in reproof "... you were passed out drunk and Sierra was beside herself."

He rolled his eyes. "I know. I'm sorry. *Geez*. How many times do I have to say it?"

Sierra put a hand on his leg, letting him know it was okay. He seemed to relax as he placed a hand over hers.

"I had a long talk with Sierra." Nadine's voice trembled as she touched her hair. "I told her you were a no-count drunk. That you would never change. That she needed to leave you and find another life."

Dalton's jaw tightened. "You're the one who persuaded her to leave me?" His voice had a dangerous edge to it.

"Yes." Moisture filled Nadine's eyes. "I even gave her the money for a fresh start. But what I failed to realize at the time is that a person can change." Her voice quivered. "I was wrong about you, Dalton. So terribly wrong. Not a day goes by that I don't regret it."

A frigid silence descended over them.

Bennie looked at Sierra. "Nadine was here the morning you called and announced that Parker was proposing."

Sierra felt Dalton tense.

"I was upset, afraid you were making a terrible mistake," Bennie continued. "I know you, Sierra, better than you know yourself. You've always loved Dalton. I said all of this to Nadine and she admitted that it was her fault you left. So we concocted a plan to get the two of you back together." Bennie shrugged, an ironic smile tipping her lips. "This whole scenario is more Jane Austen-like than you realize. But instead of *Pride and Prejudice* you've been reliving *Persuasion*, where a trusted friend convinces the heroine not to marry her true love."

A hysterical laugh rose in Sierra's mouth. She tried to hold it back, but it rumbled out. Only Bennie would do something this outrageous! "It's true." She turned to Dalton. "The heroine in *Persuasion* realizes what a foolish mistake she made at the end and goes back to her true love."

Hope lit his face, turning his eyes crystal blue. "Are you saying what I think you're saying, Sie?"

The doorbell rang.

Bennie let out a sigh. "*Jiminy Cricket*. This place is like Grand Central Station tonight." Nimbly, she hopped up to get it. She paused when she realized Sierra and Dalton were gaping at her. "Well, no sense in pretending anymore," she huffed. "I tell you one thing. It's a pain in the butt to walk with those crutches. My armpits are plumb raw."

Dalton chuckled. "I always knew your aunt was eccentric, but this is certifiably crazy."

"Tell me about it," Sierra muttered.

Bennie opened the door. Sierra heard a man's voice and then

Bennie started talking faster and more high-pitched. "Yeah, she's here. Come on in."

Sierra's heart dropped when she saw him. "Parker. W-what're you doing here?" She stumbled to her feet and gave him a stiff hug. This was the stuff nightmares were made of. She looked back at Dalton, whose lips were tight with fury. Then she looked at Parker. "H-how did you even find this place?"

"You aunt's address was listed online." He shrugged. "And well, it's a small town." He searched her face. "I would've told you I was coming, but well," he chuckled nervously, "you haven't exactly been answering my calls."

"Yeah, about that …" She looked at Dalton who was studying her with intense, brooding eyes.

Parker cleared his throat. "The time you've been away … it's been rough. And not just because you haven't been at work. I missed you, Sierra. I should've done this from the very get-go. I'm sorry it took me so long."

Her heart pounded erratically against her ribcage like a caged bird trying to escape.

Parker got down on one knee and peered up at her, adoration shining in his eyes. Then he whipped out a black box and popped it open, revealing a very large rock. "Sierra McCain. I adore you." His lips curved into a hopeful smile. "Make me the happiest man on earth. Marry me?"

Sierra was dumbfounded. She heard a grunt and looked at Dalton. His face had turned ten shades darker and he looked like he might jump up any minute and punch Parker's lights out.

"Uh, who are you?" Parker asked, looking at Dalton, suspicion coating his voice.

"Someone who's been at the party a lot longer than you, pal," Dalton retorted.

Sierra looked at Nadine, who was staring wide-eyed, shock twisting her features, like she was witnessing a train wreck. Next, she looked at Bennie, then back at Parker.

Uncertainty settled into Parker's eyes, turning them a muddy brown. "I probably shouldn't have done this here." He wet his lips, the words spilling out. "We can go back to Rossini's, and do this the right way."

In that moment, everything suddenly became clear. "But I don't want Rossini's." Sierra looked at Bennie who tipped her lips in a slight smile.

"What do you want?" There was an open challenge in Bennie's eyes.

A laugh tickled Sierra's throat. "I want pizza."

Parker's jaw went slack. "Excuse me?"

"Pizza from Clydedale's with my best friend." She looked at Dalton.

A crooked grin tugged at the corner of Dalton's lip. "Sounds good to me. Much better than those awful cucumber sandwiches." He made a gagging motion with his finger.

Sierra bubbled out a laugh, feeling a burst of joy that sent her soaring. Well, almost … She turned to Parker. "I'm sorry, but I can't marry you," she began.

He stumbled to his feet, a dazed look on his face. "I—I don't understand. Is it because I wasn't ready before? You know how hard it is on me because of my parents' divorce. And yet, I'm willing to marry you anyway."

She let out a half-laugh. She thought about how devastated she'd been when Parker hadn't proposed and how it was turning out to be the greatest blessing of her life. "No, it's not that. It's because I fell in love with someone else a long time ago. Only I'd forgotten." She looked at Bennie and Nadine, chuckling under her breath. "I just needed two old crows with one crazy, harebrained scheme to remind me."

"Careful now," Bennie warned, then broke into a smile.

A deep furrow dented Parker's brow. "You're not looking at this sensibly. The two of us are perfect together. We share the same interests, the same career, mutual friends."

She chuckled, wondering how she could've ever thought she'd be happy with Parker. "I know. By all accounts, you're the perfect guy." She offered an apologetic smile. "Just not the right one for me."

He gave her a dejected look. "I see. I guess I'll be going then."

She gave him another hug, feeling sorry for him. "I hope you have a safe trip back."

When he got to the door, he turned. "What about work? And the Pristine Pizza account?"

For Parker, work would always take precedence. And that was okay ... for someone else, but not for her. "I'll see you through that account. If you want me to, that is. Then after that." She shrugged. "Well, I guess we'll just have to see."

He nodded and went out the door. She closed it behind him, sighing in relief. "Well, that's that."

"Good riddance, city slicker," Dalton muttered, getting to his feet.

Sierra jutted her thumb. "See what I just gave up for you?"

He stepped up to her, that slow smile she loved so much easing over his lips. "I always knew that when push came to shove, you wouldn't be able to resist me," he taunted in a low, husky tone that sent shivers dancing down her spine.

A smile pulled at her lips. "You're such a cocky jerk." *And much too good looking for your own good,* she added mentally.

He cocked an eyebrow. "Is that right?" He stepped closer, sending her cells into a frenzy, her breath coming faster.

Desire simmered in her stomach to the point where she felt like she might explode. "Why don't you just shut up and kiss me?"

His beautiful eyes sparkled. "As you wish, darling."

He circled his arm around her waist, pulling her roughly to him. His lips connected with hers in a glorious rush of fiery, brilliant fireworks that sent her heart spinning wildly. They didn't pull away until they heard Bennie clear her throat.

"That's a little much for these two old crows," Bennie said dryly, fingering her neck.

Dalton kept his arms around Sierra. His eyes roved over her face like he was soaking in every detail. "You're mine, Sierra McCain."

The feeling of belonging that wafted over Sierra was as old and ageless as the venerable mansion in which they stood. "And so I am," she proclaimed joyously.

After years of searching, she'd finally found home.

EPILOGUE

Three months later ...
        Sierra gripped the steering wheel tighter and looked up at the darkening sky.

"Looks like a storm's coming in," Bennie said as if reading her mind. "But I think it'll move in and out fast."

"I don't know about that. It looks like this front's settling in for the long haul. Are you sure you still want to stop by Huntington Island? We can wait and go later." Bennie had asked Sierra to take her to Charleston to shop for clothes, but insisted on taking a detour first.

"No, I want to go today."

"Okay." Sierra sighed heavily when she saw the stubborn set of Bennie's chin. "I mean, who doesn't love going to the beach during a torrential down pour?" she pouted. "Makes perfect sense."

Bennie grunted in response.

There was no use in wasting her breath to argue because Bennie would do what she wanted anyway. A smile slid over her lips as she glanced at her strong-willed aunt. Bennie was just Bennie. There was no other way to describe her. She and Sierra would always disagree, but they'd gotten really close during the three months Sierra had been back at the mansion.

She looked at the road in front of her, her thoughts flitting over everything that had happened since she moved back to Sugar Pines. *Macbeth* was a marginal success. The production, itself, went well. They just didn't sell as many tickets as Sierra hoped. Then again, the pressure was off because Bennie really didn't need the money. As it turned out, Bennie had funded the outdoor theater using private donations, proving she was a lot sharper in business than she'd let on. Sierra was still networking with the tourist companies in the hope they could boost sales for the next production. The situation was looking promising.

True to her word, she was overseeing the Pristine Pizza account through to the end. She'd spoken to Parker a couple of times over the phone about business matters, and he was the consummate professional, cordial and reserved. Which was fine with her. The less she had to talk to him the better. She wished him well and was glad their relationship had ended amicably.

Sierra had a few interviews set up in the coming weeks with advertising agencies in Charleston. Things looked optimistic, especially with a major account like Pristine Pizza on her résumé. Dalton was worried about the commute, but it was only thirty minutes each way. He'd offered Sierra seed money to start her own agency, but she wasn't ready for that yet. Maybe in a couple of years, but not now. Too many other things were commanding her attention. Well, one thing, actually … Dalton.

A dart of warmth pinged her heart and spread through her body. Things were so wonderful with Dalton that she often had to pinch herself to make sure she wasn't dreaming. They'd taken the best parts of their relationship from before and made it into so much more. She was so in love with Dalton Chandler that she could hardly form a clear thought. He knew the effect he had on her and often teased her about it. She'd dish it right back. And around and around they went.

The night before, Dalton surprised her by showing up outside her bedroom window a little after eleven p.m. She'd opened her window to question what he was doing.

"This couldn't wait until morning," he said in a husky tone that sent delicious shivers circling down her spine. His eyes took on a smolder, then he pulled her into his arms and gave her a series of tender kisses that melted her bones and sent her heart into flips.

Afterwards, they'd climbed on her bed and watched a movie on her laptop until they drifted off to sleep. As attracted to Dalton as she was, Sierra promised herself a long time ago that she'd never again make the same mistake. She would wait until marriage to take their relationship to the next level. Dalton applauded her decision and said he had no problem taking things slow.

She frowned. How long was Dalton going to wait before proposing? At this rate, she was destined to be an old maid. Then again, it had only been three months, but she was ready—readier than she'd ever been. She wanted to start a life with Dalton ... eventually wanted children.

They turned into the entrance of the state park. Sierra pulled up to the guard station and offered a polite smile. "Hello."

The young guy looked at her and Bennie. "Just the two of you?"

"Yep."

He glanced at the sky. "It looks like rain."

Sierra arched an eyebrow, cutting her eyes at Bennie. "Sure does."

"I get the senior discount," Bennie piped in.

"Will you be going into the lighthouse?" the guard asked.

Sierra shook her head. "I don't think so."

"Yes," Bennie nearly shouted, right in her ear. *Geez.* The woman was going to burst her eardrum. She turned to Bennie. "Are you sure? There are lots of steps and with the impending rain—"

Bennie leaned over, practically laying on top of Sierra as she looked at the guard. "Yes, we'll be going to the lighthouse."

He smiled, his eyes twinkling with amusement. "That'll be $12.25. Y'all have a nice day."

Sierra paid the money and they drove through. "Are you sure you want to go to the lighthouse today?" She just had to ask once more for the record.

"Absolutely." The skin under Bennie's chin jiggled as she clamped her jaw.

"Okay." It wasn't just the rain that made Sierra hesitant to go to the lighthouse. This was her and Dalton's special spot, and she wanted her first time back to be with him. They'd been talking about going but hadn't set a time yet.

Oh, well. She'd have to just get over it because Bennie was determined to go.

They pulled into a parking space. Sierra opened the door and got out. The wind flapped against her clothes. She pushed her hair out of her eyes and waited for Bennie, but she just sat there. Sierra raised her hands. "Aren't you getting out?" Bennie was acting even stranger than usual.

Bennie opened the passenger door and stuck her head out. "It's a little windier than I realized. You go on out to the beach. I'll be right behind you." She held up her phone. "I need to call Wesley back. He's been trying to reach me all morning."

Sierra's eyes rounded. "Seriously?"

"Go on," Bennie said, shooing with her hands.

"Okay, whatever." Maybe her aunt was losing it. She looked at the beach and white-capped waves thrashing against the shore in anticipation of the approaching storm. She walked across the parking lot and through the grass. When she reached the beach, she took off her sandals. The minute her bare feet touched the sand, a thrill ran through her. She squished her toes in the grainy sand, then took a deep breath, letting the briny taste of the ocean envelope her. She'd forgotten how much she loved this place. Suddenly, she was glad Bennie insisted on coming.

Sierra felt like a kid again, her steps light and nimble, as she half-walked, half-skipped along the shore. She was the only one here. It was liberating to have the beach all to herself! She looked up at the imposing lighthouse, the bottom third white and the top black. Memories from her childhood swirled around her like a kaleidoscope. She and Dalton running on the sand, playing in the waves, exploring the shoreline, hunting for crabs. It had been right over there by those rocks in the distance where Dalton first told her he loved her.

A laugh escaped her throat as she held out her hands and twirled.

She looked out at the frothy ocean that was calling her name. Storm or not, she had to get out in it, craved being one with nature. She tossed her sandals on the sand and rolled up her jeans as high as they'd go.

She went to the edge. The water was warm and bubbly as she waded in. She leaned over and trailed her fingertips through the water, the motion of the waves swaying her body. She felt small amid all this water, stretching out to the horizon infinitely further than the eye could see. And yet at the same time, she felt large and fearless, like there was nothing she couldn't accomplish.

"They have swimsuits for that."

She gulped then spun around, her mind registering that she knew that voice as well as she knew her own. She let out a half-laugh. "Dalton? What're you doing here?"

He was standing beside the shore in a black t-shirt and rolled up jeans, barefoot. His hair was blowing in the wind. She'd never seen a better-looking man. His physique was so chiseled he could've passed for a Greek statue. An easy smile stole over his lips. "Hey, Sie."

Just like that, she was bathed in warmth. She let out a giggle, suddenly understanding why Bennie was acting so strange. "You and Bennie planned this whole thing, didn't you?"

Dalton stepped into the water, moving next to her. "I might've had a little help," he winked. He slid his arms around her waist, pulling her to him. Sierra peered into his eyes which picked up the color of the ocean. The familiar spark of desire flamed as she moistened her lips, assuming he'd kiss her. But amusement touched his features. "You were having so much fun, I hated to interrupt."

She chuckled, her cheeks going warm. "Well, I thought I was alone."

"No," he said, his voice going fierce. "I'll never leave you alone. I love you, Sierra McCain. You and only you. Body and soul."

She swallowed, emotion flowing like warm rays of blessed sunshine over her heart. "I love you too."

"The past three months have been wonderful."

"Yes, they have."

"I want you to know that I swear I'll do everything in my power to earn your trust … every day, every moment for the rest of our lives."

Tears glistened in her eyes. "You already have."

He nodded like he was internalizing what she'd said. Then a grin tugged at his lips. "Here's how this is gonna go down. We're gonna make a wager."

She rested the palms of her hands on his muscular pecs, loving the feel of his arms around her. "What's the wager?"

He looked at the restless sky. "I say the rain'll fall in ten minutes."

She pursed her lips. "Five."

His eyes twinkled. "You're on."

"Wait, you forgot to name the prize."

He cocked his head. "If I win, we get married two months from now."

She laughed, her heart doing a dance. This was really happening! She was happy, so gloriously happy!

His eyes searched hers and in them she could see the culmination of a lifetime of love. "You game, Sie?"

A smile tugged at her lips. "Let's see … what do I want." She feigned thinking even though the answer came instantly. "I know. If I win, we get married next month instead."

He broke into a large grin. "You're on."

No sooner had the words left his mouth than the first drops of rain dotted over them. A minute later, the bottom gave way as buckets came down.

"Looks like I'm the winner," she chimed over the rain.

"No, I'm the real winner because I get you," he murmured as his lips claimed hers.

Amidst the commotion around them, the bashing waves and rain, Sierra's heart found peace. Forever was now. Forever was here. She'd gone around the world on a journey to find her heart and ended up right back where she started, in the arms of her best friend.

The one she would never forget.

YOUR FREE BOOK AWAITS ...

Hey there, thanks for taking the time to read *Seeking Mr. Perfect*. If you enjoyed it, please take a minute to give me a review on Amazon. I really appreciate your feedback, as I depend largely on word of mouth to promote my books.

If you sign up for our newsletter, we will give you one of our books, Beastly Charm: A contemporary retelling of beauty & the beast, for FREE. Plus, you'll get information on discounts and other freebies. For more information, visit:

http://bit.ly/freebookjenniferyoungblood

BOOKS BY JENNIFER YOUNGBLOOD

Check out Jennifer's Amazon Page:
http://bit.ly/jenniferyoungblood

Billionaire Boss Romance
Her Blue Collar Boss
Her Lost Chance Boss

Georgia Patriots Romance
The Hot Headed Patriot
The Twelfth Hour Patriot
The Unstoppable Patriot

O'Brien Family Romance
The Impossible Groom (Chas O'Brien)
The Twelfth Hour Patriot (McKenna O'Brien)
The Stormy Warrior (Caden O'Brien and Tess Eisenhart)
Rewriting Christmas (A Novella)
Yours By Christmas (Park City Firefighter Romance)
Her Crazy Rich Fake Fiancé

Navy SEAL Romance
The Resolved Warrior
The Reckless Warrior
The Diehard Warrior
The Stormy Warrior

The Jane Austen Pact
Seeking Mr. Perfect

Texas Titan Romances
The Hometown Groom
The Persistent Groom
The Ghost Groom
The Jilted Billionaire Groom
The Impossible Groom

Get the Texas Titan Romance Collection HERE
The Perfect Catch (Last Play Series)

Hawaii Billionaire Series
Love Him or Lose Him
Love on the Rocks
Love on the Rebound
Love at the Ocean Breeze
Love Changes Everything
Loving the Movie Star
Love Under Fire (A Companion book to the Hawaii Billionaire Series)

Kisses and Commitment Series
How to See With Your Heart

Angel Matchmaker Series
Kisses Over Candlelight
The Cowboy and the Billionaire's Daughter

Romantic Thrillers
    False Identity
    False Trust
    Promise Me Love
    Burned

Contemporary Romance
    Beastly Charm

Fairytale Retellings (The Grimm Laws Series)
    Banish My Heart **(This book is FREE)**
    The Magic in Me
    Under Your Spell
    A Love So True

Southern Romance
    Livin' in High Cotton
    Recipe for Love

The Second Chance Series
    Forgive Me (Book 1)
    Love Me (Book 2)

Short Stories
    The Southern Fried Fix

ABOUT JENNIFER YOUNGBLOOD

Jennifer loves reading and writing clean romance. She believes that happily ever after is not just for stories. Jennifer enjoys interior design, rollerblading, clogging, jogging, and chocolate. In Jennifer's opinion there are few ills that can't be solved with a warm brownie and scoop of vanilla-bean ice cream.

Jennifer grew up in rural Alabama and loved living in a town where "everybody knows everybody." Her love for writing began as a young teenager when she wrote stories for her high school English teacher to critique.

Jennifer has BA in English and Social Sciences from Brigham Young University where she served as Miss BYU Hawaii in 1989. Before becoming an author, she worked as the owner and editor of a monthly newspaper named *The Senior Times*.

She now lives in the Rocky Mountains with her family and spends her time writing and doing all of the wonderful things that make up the life of a busy wife and mother.

facebook.com/authorjenniferyoungblood

twitter.com/authorjenn1

instagram.com/authorjenniferyoungblood

Made in the USA
San Bernardino,
CA

58870913R00112